THE INCANDESCENT ONES

Other books by the authors:

FRED HOYLE

    Frontiers of Astronomy
    The Nature of the Universe
    **Nicolaus Copernicus: An Essay on His Life and
       Work**
    October the First Is Too Late

FRED HOYLE AND GEOFFREY HOYLE

    The Inferno
    Into Deepest Space
    The Molecule Men

THE INCANDESCENT ONES

FRED HOYLE

AND

GEOFFREY HOYLE

EDITED BY BARBARA HOYLE

HARPER & ROW, PUBLISHERS
NEW YORK, HAGERSTOWN
SAN FRANCISCO
LONDON

FIRST EDITION

Designed by Gloria Adelson

Library of Congress Cataloging in Publication Data

Hoyle, Fred, Sir.
   The incandescent ones.
   I. Hoyle, Geoffrey, joint author. II. Title.
PZ4.H8675Im3   [PR6058.098]   823'.9'14   76-47254
ISBN 0-06-011956-X

77 78 79 80 10 9 8 7 6 5 4 3 2 1

For Donald and Mary Shane

THE INCANDESCENT ONES

The spin-off of discoveries from the Dark Ages penetrated even to the Slavic World.
These were the words with which it all started. Spoken by Professor Ortov of Moscow University.

"The spin-off of discoveries from the Dark Ages . . ." Not the sort of thing you'd ever say by mistake. Ortov knew what he was saying but he didn't know to whom it was said. It was a code address signal to a member of his class of some two hundred students who were attending his lectures on the art forms of Byzantium.

The lectures were held at 8 A.M. on cold, dark January mornings on the twenty-seventh floor of the University building, an ancient mausoleum dating from the Stalin period, before the oppressive regime in Russia really gained a firm hold on the people.

I'd risen about 7 A.M. in my dorm at the student hostel to which I'd been assigned the preceding September. Rolling with a groan off my half-metre-wide bed, with its apology of a mattress, and negotiating a bare feminine leg protruding from a nearby bed, I made my way to the showers.

Instead of working on the steady-droplet principle of an American shower, all the water came down on your head in a simple deluge, operating in the manner of a flush lavatory. You simply stood underneath a hole, pulled a piece of string, and down it all came—cold.

I was still gasping by the time I'd dressed, but at least I was fully awake and prepared for the day. Arriving early at the canteen safely ensured my securing a piece of bread and a bowl of sour milk. Ten minutes later I was on my way to Professor Ortov's lecture, arriving eventually at the twenty-seventh floor, after the usual cattle-truck exercise on the elevators.

Actually, I'd soon come to prefer lectures at eight o'-clock in the morning, because the classrooms had less of a smell about them at that time of day. The girls, chubby things mostly, but with a few hard-muscled ones mixed among them, used to sit predominantly to one side of the room; and the Russian men, not being interested at 8 A.M., sat at the other side. Being American, and therefore different in my habits, I sat among the girls. But in truth I didn't have too much of an eye for them, even the muscly ones, because I had to keep a close watch on Professor Ortov, a man of solid stature in his middle fifties, with a shock of pepper-and-salt hair and a mouthful of big teeth. I kept watch on Professor Ortov, not because I was overly interested in the art forms of Byzantium, but because of what he might say. Week after week, I listened for it:

"The spin-off of discoveries . . ."

In my capacity as a rookie agent, I'd been told just one big thing—to listen for this phrase, and, should I hear it, to purchase two books of my choice on the same day at 1.30 P.M. from the university bookstore. Pretty slim equipment for an agent—rookie or otherwise. Yet step by step, with remorseless logic, these seemingly trifling instructions were to make me the plaything, not just of the intelligence agencies of both West and East, but of a third agency whose very existence I was still entirely unaware of. *Multum in parvo.*

I was brought up by my father. Although children in my position are supposed to suffer in later life from a one-parent syndrome, if I did I was certainly not conscious of it. Indeed, my early life was anything but monotonous or withdrawn. My father's name was Anaxagoras, which I understood to have been the name of his paternal grandfather, a priest of the Russian Orthodox Church. But people in our hometown of Ketchum, Idaho, had little use for it. They called my pop Alexei, or just plain Alex.

When I was young, my father spent ten years working in the Moscow office of the U.S. trade association, thus putting to effective use his knowledge of the Russian language, which, as he often told me, he had learned as a first-generation immigrant from his Russian parents. And I too had become a fluent speaker of Russian, from accompanying my father when he took up the trade post. In fact, I was brought up in Moscow from the age of three to thirteen.

From Moscow we returned to Ketchum, which was certainly some difference in life style. Ketchum, I might say, small place that it is, is one of the largest collection points in the United States. But, unlike Moscow, for sheep, not people. It is also near to Sun Valley, which was important to my father, for he was a keen skier of a high-grade amateur class. However, by the time I was fifteen he had to give me best on the slopes, much to his seeming regret. To the time of his disappearance, we often made mountain expeditions together. Indeed, it was from these boyhood trips that I developed my passion for open-mountain skiing, the kind of thing which sets the normal prepared-slope artist's teeth on edge. For good reason. I was always suffering minor injuries, which three or four years later went a long way towards keeping me out of the U.S. national ski team. I suppose the bangs and bruises knocked a fraction of a second off my timings, but this was the least part of it. It was rather that, whenever the national trials came up, I always seemed to be either hobbling around or to have one arm in a sling. Even so, I could not keep away from the wide clean snowfields of the big mountains. Nor could my father. One day, when I was coming up sixteen, he did not return from a solitary expedition among the hills.

Thereafter, I was boarded away at high school for upwards of a year, a painful, fretful, and solitary year, from which I escaped at last by enrolling at the early age of seventeen at the University of Washington. This I did by putting myself down as a student of the Russian language and literature, which made life easy for me. No trouble getting good grades with plenty of time to spare, while others sweated through their courses.

During winter vacations I worked as a ski instructor, and during the summer I took to the water, offering instructions in the art of water skiing to those willing to pay for my services. As I look back over this period, I can now see one or two somewhat unusual aspects to it. At the time, however, I was quite unaware of any oddity. While I had many acquaintances at the University, unlike most other students I failed to make any close friends. While outwardly I seemed approachable, I was in fact a bit of a loner.

Students of the liberal arts, like me, were required to take a science course at some stage of their university careers. This requirement was much dreaded, and most chose astronomy or earth-science as the least unpalatable alternative. Perversely I chose physics, and surprisingly I got an A grade in it. I was pleased, in a boyish kind of way, thinking nothing further of it.

Most American universities like their foreign-language students to spend a semester at least, better a year, in the country where the main language of study is actually spoken. So in my senior year, when I reached a suitably advanced stage in my work, I wrote the Dean's office with the proposal that I should spend a year at Moscow University. This was agreed to in the late spring, with my entry scheduled for the coming fall.

On my side, there was nothing devious in this arrangement. The deviousness only began when I was called to an interview, ostensibly to discuss my visit to Russia. I was surprised to find, not the instructor to whom I was accustomed, but a more senior professor of Slavonic studies, a man well known in scholastic circles. It was he who advised me to attend Professor Ortov's lectures. Then, in a grave tone of voice, to my very considerable astonishment, he suggested it would be a useful service to my country if, while in Russia, I were to undertake a small straightforward task. Should the learned Professor Ortov, with his pepper-and-salt hair and his mouthful of big teeth, use a certain phrase, then on that same day, at 1.30 P.M. precisely, I was to purchase two books from the Moscow University bookstore. Nothing more. *Multum in parvo,* as I said before.

For this service I was to receive a financial consideration, a kind of honorarium as one might say. In my chronically impoverished condition, this seemed a persuasive argument. I expected to receive a few hundred dollars, and this I would happily have spent. But when a few days later I found five thousand dollars had been paid to my account at the First National of Seattle I was much too scared to touch it at all. Not that I was frightened physically. It was more I had the feeling that someone was trying to buy my soul.

One reason I would have been glad of a bit of money to spend would have been to enjoy the last of the winter's snow by myself, without needing to work as an instructor. To give an idea of the kind of thing I would have been happy to avoid, one day at the ski center I was sitting in the instructor's office enjoying a cup of coffee when my attention was riveted by an exceedingly loud tread of boots on the wooden floor outside. Thinking a veritable giant was bearing down on me, I glanced up to see a small grey-haired, round-faced man, pince-nez stuck on a sharp nose, appear at the office door. He wore a windbreaker bearing the monogram of the Maryland Sno' Skeeters. His boots continued to beat a murderous tattoo on the floor as he advanced on me with outstretched hand.

"Edelstam," he announced with an apologetic air.

It did not take the wisdom of Solomon to foresee that this little man, with his pince-nez and leaden gait, was not going to be the success of the year on the slopes. In fact, he was quite shockingly bad. His ineptness was made the more painful to me by the profuse thanks he offered for the few inadequate bits of advice I was asked to give him. Even after a long hour and a half of it, I still could not escape, for he insisted on buying me a sandwich—because earlier he had interrupted my cup of coffee. While we ate, he showed me pictures of his wife and daughter, and of his home in Maryland. The wife was much the same as himself, but the daughter was a healthy, strong-looking young woman with short hair, wide-set eyes, and dimpled cheeks. Odd that this girl could be the offspring of such a thumping, clumping fellow. But nature somehow contrives to shuffle us all around in a remarkable way, a fact I'd already noticed quite a few times before. At last my Sno' Skeeter was gone, and I was left lamenting the loss of the best part of one of my few remaining late spring days among the snows.

This short sketch of my early years by no means tells all, but it gives quite enough, I think, up to the September day when I arrived once more in Russia. In my capacity as a rookie agent I had received no training, nor any further instruction, and the five thousand dollars still lay untouched in my account at the First National of Seattle.

After Professor Ortov's lecture, the morning dragged by without my being able to give any real attention to what was going on around me. The lunch break came at last, and I found a vacant seat in the canteen and there consumed a small pot of Turkish coffee. At 1.10 P.M. I started on my way to the bookstore. I had decided already on two titles which it was reasonable for a student in my position to buy, but I wanted to have a few minutes' time in hand, so as to go through the motions of seeming to select the two books.

In a style which I felt to be neither too hasty nor yet too leisurely, I made my choices from the bookstore shelves. The girl clerk on duty at the purchase desk was one I had not seen there before. I had made several previous visits, not too many—I hadn't haunted the place or anything like that—but enough so that I believed I knew all the desk clerks by sight. But this one was either new or she had escaped my previous investigations. She was about five

7

feet six in height, with shining dark hair, and with brown wide-set eyes. Dimples appeared in her cheeks as she spoke. The language was native Russian.

A voice at my elbow, a clear, resonant English voice, English not American, asked, "I wonder, sir, if I might presume to ask for your help? I am looking for Kransky's *Life of Pushkin.*"

The man had light hair and eyes, the eyes clear and hard. He was tallish, maybe six feet one, and spare of build. Although he didn't move much, I had the strong impression of firm muscle and of an athletic constitution. This assessment was of a kind I was well used to making, from my years of experience as an instructor. In that job you were always on the look-out for the rare client with a high physical capacity, because you could do a lot more with him, which was a relief from so many of the others, like the Sno' Skeeter from Maryland. This fellow was about thirty-five, I would say, old for a student, if he was a student. I translated his request to the girl. With a dimpled apology to me for stopping packing my books, she took them away with her as she went off to find a copy of Kransky's *Life of Pushkin.*

"Been in Russia long?" I asked.

"A few days. I've been coming here, on and off, for quite a number of years. A friend asked me to pick up a copy of this Kransky book."

"Your friend reads Russian?"

"Hardly be of much use to him if he didn't, would it?"

I felt the Englishman to be consciously studying me with his cold blue eyes, and I myself, sensing this business was going to be far less simple than I had imagined, was acutely aware of everything about him, to a point where

I would be in no difficulty to recognise him should we ever meet again.

Then the girl was back, with my parcel neatly wrapped, and with a copy of the *Life of Pushkin* in the other hand, which she handed to the Englishman. I paid for my two purchases, fascinated again by the dimples in the girl's face. I wondered if I was supposed to make some mention of the homestead back in good old Maryland, but with the Englishman still hovering nearby, I decided against it. So with what I hoped was a noncommittal nod, I simply took my leave.

An hour later I unpacked the parcel, quite openly in a small cubicle at the reading room of the main University library. The package contained three books. The one I hadn't bought was the *Life of Pushkin* by Alexander Kransky.

I was of course aware that an 'incident' had just taken place, but it quite defeated my imagination to understand what the incident might portend. Indeed I would be prepared to state that the full subtlety and counter-subtlety of what had just transpired in full public view back there in the bookstore would probably have baffled even the most experienced of agents. That some form of interchange of books might have taken place was reasonably obvious. On the face of it, I was at the losing end of the interchange, if there had been one, for when I examined my copy of Kransky there was nothing unusual about it. Quickly I ran through all the pages. No passages in it had been marked, no words were underlined, nothing obvious and silly like that. No student's comments in the margin, as there might have been if the wide-eyed girl with the dimples had chosen to give me a secondhand copy. I even took the trouble to fetch the library's own Kransky from the shelves. It was just the same as the one I had.

Nor was there anything loose within the book itself, except a leaflet advertising the current exhibition at the Pushkin Museum. But since there were similar leaflets in the other two books, and presumably in all the books now being sold at the store, what was there in this? And still, there it was, two copies of the *Life of Pushkin,* and now three leaflets about the Pushkin Museum. Perhaps the message was for me to attend the exhibition at the Museum. But, if so, why were the instructions not more explicit? Particularly, at what time, on what day?

For maybe an hour or more I mulled the situation over in my mind. If I was being expected at the Museum, it was natural to assume that recognition would be left to someone else. Obviously I couldn't be expected to hang about the Museum for long periods, so there had to be answers to the day, and to the time of day. The only time of day ever mentioned to me was 1.30 P.M., but at the bookstore. Yet it seemed a fair inference that a similar time might be intended at the Museum also—there seemed no other possibility. Which day? Well, certainly not today, because it was already approaching 3.30 P.M. Of the days ahead, only tomorrow had any kind of uniqueness about it. So tomorrow it had to be, if there was anything at all in the Pushkin idea.

The following day at 1.30 P.M. found me at the Museum examining an example of early Bolshevik art. I stood below a huge wall painting showing a swirling parade of workers and peasants carrying banners. Behind them chugged the first tractor to till the fertile fields of the motherland. Great stuff, if you had the stomach for it. Under my right arm I carried my copy of the *Life of*

Pushkin, a touch of bright inspiration, I thought, in welcome contrast to the drab mediocrity of this awful exhibition.

A party of young Russian schoolchildren raced and chattered around me, with an elderly harassed man, seemingly their teacher, seeking to set limits to their exuberance. Suddenly I was hit from behind, and my book fell from the light, nonchalant grasp in which I had been holding it. The considerable weight of Kransky, and the momentum it gained in the fall, caused the book to slide for quite a way on the polished marble floor.

"There, see what you've done," admonished the teacher. "Didn't I say you would be making trouble? If the attendant sees you . . ."

So he went on, until a smiling little girl came up to me with the book.

"Sorry, sir," she said with a curtsey.

"That's all right." I smiled in return, clutching the book more firmly now. A Museum official appeared, and the teacher immediately shepherded his flock into a tighter, more disciplined group.

"There, didn't I say . . ." I heard him repeat, as the group passed on quickly to a nearby room.

I glanced at the book. It said *Life of Pushkin* all right, and the author was still Alexander Kransky. Only it wasn't my book. The weight of it was slightly different. Later I was to find that the end part of it had been cut away, to be replaced by a compartment constructed to give the whole book just the same size as before. Aware of the difference, I suddenly lost my nonchalance. Feeling awkwardly conspicuous, I left the Museum with a curious fluttering going on somewhere inside me.

Even with this further piece of the puzzle now in place,

I was no nearer a proper understanding of what had happened. Imagine an express train thundering through a complex crossing of many lines. The casual bystander has no initial knowledge of exactly on what line, in what direction, the train will eventually emerge from its many crossing points. But the signalman who sets the points expects to know. So indeed did two large, powerful intelligence agencies believe they knew precisely how events would run, since they believed themselves to have now set all the relevant crossing points. Yet very soon there would be developments that would run quite elsewhere, guided differently by hidden hands.

During the afternoon I pondered the problem of where to examine my new copy of the *Life of Pushkin*. Sly glances in public at the thing gave no answer at all. So where? Not in the classroom, nor in the always over-crowded library reading room. My own room? The trouble was that in Russia there was no such thing as one's own room, at any rate for a student like me. In the public toilets? Not on your life. The K.G.B. was known to have agents covering every toilet in Moscow.

I solved the problem by using the hostel dormitory, not by day—too many people around. So I waited until the midnight hour, when one of my neighbours was at work with his girl friend. The normal practice was for the rest of the dormitory to wait for the girl's first whimper, then for us all to join in, so that by the time the girl reached her orgasm the whole place was a regular pandemonium of moans and groans. It was then that I opened up the secret compartment in my new copy of Kransky's *Life of Pushkin*.

I transferred its contents to my briefcase. The following

day it was possible to glance quite freely through the briefcase, without actually taking out the contents. Riffling through one's papers during a lecture was a frequently performed operation.

The compartment in the book had contained a railroad ticket from Moscow to Erevan, Armenia, with a stopover at Topolev, Georgia. It also had contained two maps, one a town map of Topolev, on which a particular exit road had been marked with a red cross. The other was a map of the surrounding district, from which I found that the marked road led to a small town called Strogoff some eighty kilometres from Topolev. I also found a student travel permit and money. Not a great deal of money, but just about what a student would be expected to carry.

I'd made quite a few acquaintances in the University, but none was close enough to worry too much if I was away for a week or two. So on the evening of the day following my encounter in the Museum I packed a few odds and ends into a small Russian-made case, not at all the sort of case you would use for a long journey, and then I took the subway from the University into the city. There were dense crowds of people, both on the subway itself and at the railway terminus at which I alighted, so I judged it most unlikely that I could have been followed successfully. Since I already had a ticket, it was unnecessary to expose myself in the queue at the booking office. All in all, I thought it likely that I had managed to make a clear start.

The train rattled, roared, rumbled, and stumbled its way south. For the first thirty-six hours of the journey I stood jammed in a corridor with other poor unfortunates. To relieve the boredom, I'd buy food and drink at stations where the train stopped. But, as the journey progressed, the stops became fewer, bringing upon me great pangs of hunger. Then, as if someone had heard my stomach complaining, the stops became more frequent again. The chance to walk but a few steps on the platform of each station relieved some of the weariness I felt from the seemingly endless standing.

At first I envied the people with seats and with packages of food, who started by enjoying every moment of the journey. Yet as time went on I knew their backsides to be aching excruciatingly from the iron-hard seats. To combat the ever-growing tiredness, I frequently performed a few exercises, so by the time the station of Topolev arrived I was in surprisingly fair trim.

The train pulled laboriously from the platform, leaving me standing in a biting wind. I saw no point in delay. My instructions, for what they were worth, told me to make my way to Strogoff. I toyed for a time with the problem of whether to make straight for my destination or to spend a night at the local student hostel. A night's rest was appealing, but I knew that my presence, once known to the authorities, would make travelling to Strogoff difficult, for they'd want to know what I was up to. This consideration suggested that I should move on straightaway, if transport could be found.

After tramping the streets of Topolev, I found at last the main bus depot. Then, as though to agree with my decision, it turned out that a vehicle was due to leave for Strogoff sometime during the next few hours. With lightening heart I headed for the waiting area, out of doors of course, which was good, because it was easier to avoid observation that way. My second stroke of luck was to find room on a bench. Country folk huddled around me, sternly refusing to admit by a single shiver that it was bloody cold.

A woman two places from me sat there, in her cloth headgear, shrunken and wizened. I marvelled that in Georgia everyone is supposed to live to the right side of a hundred and thirty. The reason, I could only suppose, was that people in these parts must be given to breathing very slowly.

My good fortune seemed to be lasting, for on the bus I again found a seat. It was one of the last vacant places, being on the central aisle. We bounced, rolled, and pitched for some fifty kilometres before the bus made a series of stops, not near habitations, but in the open countryside. At one of these stops, a thickset man, wrapped in a multitude of garments, lurched past me, stabbing his hand hard into my back. Here we go, I muttered to myself, following the fellow out into the cold of the darkening day. The snow on the road was hard. At each step I took, as I followed at some distance behind the striding figure of the man from the bus, my shoes made a high-pitched squeaking sound.

We covered perhaps a couple of kilometres at quite a pace, then a rough track appeared to our left. The man in front never deviated from the road or varied in his pace. He simply waved an arm in the direction of the track. I stopped to watch the figure in front of me slowly melt into the distance. With great caution I then surveyed the way on my left. There was no sign that the track had been recently used. This was both good and bad—good because it meant that nobody had been on the track within the last few hours, and bad because my footprints would stand out on the unmarked surface. I proceeded gingerly along, trying to keep the loose snow from falling over the tops of my shoes.

Suddenly I felt very foolish. Here I was in the depth of the Russian countryside, not knowing where I was or where I was going. The more I thought about it, the more ridiculous the whole affair seemed to be. And the further I went, the colder my feet became, and the more the chill of the air seemed to cut clean through my thin overcoat. Perhaps the detail which made me feel most uncomfortable was the cheap papier-maché case I was carrying. What manner of person would be walking a remote country track with such an absurd thing? Then for the first time in my life I felt the breath-catching sensation of real fear. Gone was the self-assurance of but an hour ago, gone the glib young man of the ski slopes.

I slowed to a leaden crawl, eyeing a piece of woodland ahead with suspicion. It was only after a careful scrutiny in the failing daylight of each tree at the perimeter of the wood that I convinced myself there wasn't a sinister dark figure waiting behind every one of them. I tried turning my thoughts inwards, but nothing sufficed to remove the formless fears of my imagination. Yet I managed to creep forwards, impelled by some inner driving impulse, as if, like a computer, I had been programmed to do this thing, as if I had a desire to know what lay beyond my own imagination. In the mountains I had always loved unbroken virgin snow. Others would fight shy of descents across uncharted slopes. But to avoid them was not within my will, just as the forces within me now decreed that I must move step by step along this ever-darkening forest track.

A voice boomed on the cold air.

"Thank God, you're here at last," it said in Russian. With a strong sense of bathos, I still couldn't prevent my heart from pounding in my ears. From the side of the track lurched a man whom I recognised as the elderly teacher from the Pushkin Museum. Gone was the henlike quality with which he had then tended his flock of children.

"You're late," he said, his dark eyes flashing with animation, or was there fear in them too?

"So what?" I answered tersely.

"You don't have time to be late," came the simple reply, as he pointed the way into the wood.

I followed close on his heels, not sure what to make of it all. In front of us stood a second man. He carried with him an assortment of thermal clothes, a rifle, and large back pack.

"What's the deal?" I asked.

"You'd better change into these. I just said there isn't much time."

My spirits suddenly rose as I looked over the white fur suit I was handed, and at the heavy boots, skis, the rifle, ammunition, and survival kit which lay there on the ground.

As I dressed I studied the two men. Not much to be deduced from their worn-out appearance. The man from the Museum seemed almost to be hiding inside his fur hat and coat.

"You'll be meeting your contact in a moment," he went on. "It is imperative that you move off immediately towards the Russo-Turkish frontier. Your contact is in great danger. Every moment lost makes the danger worse."

"I can imagine," I answered.

"One thing you need to know. The Englishman you saw in the bookstore. He is not your friend."

"And the girl with the dimples?"

"That you do not need to know. It is never an advantage to know too much."

"Especially about my friends?"

"Yes, about your friends, particularly."

"What happens after crossing the frontier?"

"You will be met, provided you find the correct place to cross into Turkey. Here are your maps."

I stopped dressing for a moment to watch, as the man traced a finger across the map. I looked at the route he'd indicated for several seconds until it was firmly imprinted in my mind, then I took the map which he proffered.

"Fine," I said. "Why this route?"

"It has not been used before."

"Why not?"

"Because it is difficult and is only possible for a few people like yourself, people with exceptional qualities in skiing."

"Can my contact make it?"

"I think he may need your help."

"Is there anything special I need to know? About the route I mean."

"On the far side of the frontier it is very steep indeed, but there is said to be a traverse leading down safely on your right hand."

By this time I had finished dressing. I stowed the many items of equipment into the large pack, letting the two men stand impatiently watching. Then the three of us set off through the trees. Eventually we came to a clearing, where two tracked vehicles were standing. Now I understood why there had been no footprints on the open path from the road to the wood. My companions had come there under the cover of the forest itself.

We stopped at one of the vehicles. Three more men got out from its warmth and shelter and came towards us. Two were Russians, but I hardly noticed them, for my attention was overwhelmed by the third figure. I stood there, sucking in cold, dry air, with the hair prickling on the nape of my neck. Incredibly, the third figure was my father. There was no doubt at all about it. He rushed to me. "Peter! Peter!" he cried, thumping me on the back. Then with tears in his eyes he broke the embrace. "What a husky young brute you have become," he added in pride.

My friend from the Pushkin Museum had repeatedly emphasised the need for haste. But I felt it would be ridiculous to leave the shelter of the trees, committing us to crossing unknown country in the dark. Skiing by touch rather than by sight was something I'd tried a few times before, and I'd always hated it. In my present unfit condition, with a heavy load and with my father no complete expert, the attempt would be suicidal, only to be thought of if we were under immediate threat, which we were not. In any case, it wasn't hard to see that the real urgency was for the others to be on their way, not for my father and me.

The tracked vehicles were remarkably silent as they started up. Within moments the two of us were left alone there in the last flicker of the winter afternoon, the wind making a rushing sound as it stirred the needles of the evergreens.

I thought it advisable to move a few hundred yards

away from the spot where the vehicles had been standing, mainly to ensure that no inquisitive patrol could come on us, by the simple expedient of following the tracks left in the snow by our friends. Then the two of us set about building a snow igloo, an operation we had done many times before, during my boyhood. Once inside its welcome shelter, I broached the food and the flasks of hot liquid which my father had stored away, for I was ravenously hungry. In truth, my hunger had been more than sufficient reason to persuade me to pitch camp immediately.

While I ate, my father plied me with questions, mostly about recent events. Events since my visit to the Museum.

"You did well, Peter," he said at length, after I'd finished telling him of the train journey, and of the hour or two spent in Topolev. "I think you have given us a good start," he added.

"Why couldn't our man from the Museum simply have brought me here himself?" I asked.

"He had other things to do. There are not too many of us, you see."

I didn't see at all. Western Intelligence must have plenty of agents, I thought. When I said so, my father simply said, "There will be ample time to explain later, Peter. You must be tired after such a hard journey."

I had slipped into my lightweight thermal bag, and with the food now warm inside me, I was already struggling to keep awake. So, nothing loath, I laid my head down, and within seconds it seemed the mists of sleep gathered around me. I suppose it was the return to the ways of my boyhood which enabled me to relax in this way, so soon after finding my father to be alive and well.

In the first faint light of dawn we ate the last of the prepared food, and we swallowed the last drop of available liquid. For food from here on we would need to melt the snow, and then mix the water with one or other of the dehydrated food powders with which my pack had been well stuffed. Without the need now for this heating and melting operation, we were soon clipping on skis, picking up our loads, and poling our way in a westerly direction through the trees. Gliding in silence, we came within about an hour to the edge of a shallow open valley, leading in the distance to rising foothills.

"Better be sure of our bearings before going any further," I said, coming to a stop.

There was a compass in the breast pocket of my suit. Together we consulted the map I had been given. Although the scale was too small to show much detail, it was sufficient to give us a general guide to the terrain and direction. Satisfied that we had the right aiming point in the distance, we lifted our packs again with a grunt, and moved to cross over to the far side of the valley. The day passed by, as so many days had passed in years long gone by. I choked back a host of questions in my mind, knowing full well that my father would only unburden himself of necessary information in his own good time. This was the way it always had been.

Our passage through the upland countryside of the Republic of Georgia was by no means sporty. We made no steep downward swoops in the fashion of the eagle. Just a grinding progression through forest and glade, over undulating but rising contours. This lack of dramatic quality suited me well, actually. It gave just what I needed, exercise without too much stress. I think both of us felt the same way about it. Although I particularly remember crossing a frozen stream, where the farther bank of snow had the first spring flowers pushing upwards towards the sun, most of the details of this section of the journey became blurred into a flat continuum.

I expected my father to have fuel and a cooking stove in his pack, since my own was gorged with dehydrated foods—when two people travel cross-country together, it is usual for one to carry the food and the other the cooking equipment. Yet to my surprise my father's pack turned out to contain little but a strange largish iridescent object. The object was not of any simple geometrical shape. No straight lines dominated its surface. Nor was it spherical, or even partially spherical, in its form. Even so, I had an immediate impression of rational order about the shape of it, as if in some curious way I understood its purpose. On the first evening of our journey my father had taken it from his pack with almost a sly gesture. Then he packed snow hard into a square metal tin, pressing the snow until it was almost turned to ice. Suddenly a glow appeared around the pan, and in a flash there was liquid water, hot to the touch, within the pan. At the same instant the iridescence around the strange object increased in its intensity, into a pearly white glow. A moment later the glow was gone.

"It's a form of battery," said my father.

"But can it last us?" I asked, aware of the quick running-down of storage batteries.

"It would go on performing this function for many billions of years" was the surprising answer.

Another piece of the puzzle jolted into place. A battery of this unheard-of capacity would be worth a king's ransom. Perhaps this was why it had become so urgent to get my father and this remarkable piece of technology out of

Russia into the Western world. Inexperienced as I was in science, I needed no great inventiveness to see a host of important uses to which the thing might be put.

The days passed by more and more quickly, as they settled into a uniform routine. At night there was usually a sharp frost, which made the snow conditions good during the morning hours. But by midday even the February sun at this southern latitude was strong enough to soften the surface. By about 2 P.M. conditions worsened to a point where the progress-to-effort ratio became scarcely worthwhile. With our heavy packs, the upward grades in soft snow were becoming tolerably strenuous. So we took to halting for the day in the middle of the afternoon, which gave us plenty of time to build our nightly igloo, and then to melt water and cook food before the coming of darkness.

At last one early afternoon we came clear above the seemingly endless forest. From the map we knew this meant that we were approaching the frontier itself. Moreover, we could now see jagged rock turrets rising out of the snowfields towards the west. With the thought that from here on things would be different, we decided to make camp at this upper margin of the woodland.

The weather the following morning was exactly right for continuing into the open ground ahead, a leaden sky with a light snowfall following a warmer night than usual. The snow would soon fill our tracks. We eased our ski bindings before setting out on what we knew would be an unavoidably toilsome part of the journey. As always, we carefully buried all evidence of our presence, sweeping new snow with our skis over the top of the camp spot, and then landscaping it with a tolerable measure of skill.

While winter snow generally becomes harder the higher you go, the same rule by no means applies during the spring, because spring blizzards deposit thick blankets of soft new snow on the high ground. So it was with us now. Gone was the clean, crisp footing of previous mornings. Today we wallowed in it, and as we slowly gained height the snow fell faster, making both the going and the visibility worse and worse. By early afternoon, however, the long uphill slope thankfully eased out into a snow plateau, which had a vast look about it in the vague grey light.

I stopped, waiting for my father to come up the last bit of the incline. Time passed by, and I became worried, particularly as I could now hear a high-pitched bee-like buzz rising above the moan of the wind. Hurriedly I slung off my pack, unfastening the straps that held the rifle. Just then a figure appeared from out of the swirling snow. From its posture, with the head down against the wind, I guessed it had to be my father, and it was.

"Do you hear it?" I called.

My father stopped. I could see he was panting hard as he cocked an ear. Suddenly he nodded. With a convulsive lurch we both set off at right angles to our earlier line of progress. But only for a couple of hundred yards or so. Then we broke out of our ski bindings and began to dig furiously into the snow. As soon as we had a hole deep enough, we scooped all our belongings, packs, skis and the rifle into it. Then we burrowed ourselves as deeply as we could. It was the infra-red sensors we were afraid of, sensors that would pick up a warm exposed human body from a distance of a kilometre or more.

The noise increased, until it became a veritable roar as

a patrol of huge tank-like snowcats in line abreast passed our position. We waited for perhaps half an hour after they had gone before gingerly emerging from our entombed state. Slowly we retrieved our possessions.

"That was much too close," I gasped, looking over the plateau to where I could see great tracks churned up by the vehicles.

"Looking for us?" my father asked.

"Either that or we're nearer the frontier than I thought. Since they went straight past us without making any special search, I'm inclined to think it was only a routine frontier patrol. Especially as this plateau is just the sort of place they would use."

My father said nothing further until we had made camp, which we did after crossing the plateau. Then he asked again,

"Peter, how much longer will it take to the pass?"

"The day after tomorrow I reckon. We still have to make about ten kilometres to the south before we cross the big dividing ridge."

"Then it is time for me to speak. Perhaps I was wrong not to have spoken before."

It had always been this way. My father would tell me things in his own good time. It had always been useless to try to hurry him.

"Peter," my father went on, "I am not coming with you across this pass."

"But then why . . ."

"Why have I come so far?"

"Yes."

"To prepare the way before you."

This had the sort of religious, Biblical sound, which I

well remembered of my father. Something to do with his grandfather, I thought, the one who had been a priest in the Orthodox Church.

"I don't see how you can find your way back from here," I said firmly.

"There is a safer and surer way back for me."

"Safer than the pass?"

"Yes, much safer than the pass. It is for you alone to cross the pass."

My father tapped his head.

"I see this pass, Peter, and I tell you it is not a place for me."

I thought my father must have some knowledge of the place.

"You want me to take the battery across? Is that it?"

"That is it."

I thought for a while, and was then suddenly overwhelmed, partly by sorrow and partly by anger.

"If you think I'm going to leave you here, just for the sake of this damn thing . . ."

I stopped and pointed to my father's pack. He put an arm on my shoulder and said gravely, "Peter, you think always as a human."

It was on the tip of my tongue to ask in what other way I might think, when the implication struck me as a dark inner blow. I think I knew what was to follow, but I let my father go on.

"I'm surprised at you, Peter. Surprised you do not understand."

"Understand what?"

"That you and I are different."

"Different?"

"Peter, you and I are Outlanders."

26

As if in sudden faintness, I collapsed on top of my thermal bag, resting my head on my pack. Already in the first flash of coherent thought, I knew that my father's astonishing announcement just had to be right. Small strange aspects of my life jumped into clearer focus. Doctors had always remarked on my insensitivity to pain. They had complimented me on my exceptional speed of recovery from injuries. My easy A grade for physics was another detail. The 'loner' complex which I knew to lie deep within me was something more than a detail. My emotional reactions to situations never quite matched those of other people. I would feel deeply about things which left my acquaintances cold, and the other way around too. It was all consistent. Instead of trying to fight my father's statement, I wondered why I hadn't understood it before.

Yet this revelation seemed to raise bigger problems than it solved. I knew how humans, in their overwhelming greed for energy, had run themselves out of accessible fissile material by wantonly burning it before a satisfactory breeder technology had been developed. This was more than two hundred years ago now, in the early twenty-first century. I knew how, as decay spread everywhere over human institutions, the Outlanders had come to the Earth, supplying power beams to both major political blocs, the so-called West and East. And I knew how, by exploiting the threat to cut off one or other of the political blocs, they had enforced an unprecedented peace upon the world. Prevented from indulging in hot war, humans had then given themselves over to a perpetual and unrelenting cold war, and to fierce international competition in all forms of sport. I understood now why I had never made the U.S. ski team. The minor injuries which always seemed to prevent my attending national

the control again, wouldn't you? You could simply cut off the power beams."

"The 'thing' as you call it, is indestructible. Besides, I would not destroy it, even if it were possible to do so."

"Why?" I asked, thinking I would be glad to have my father quit speaking in riddles.

"Because it would break faith with the dead" was the still more incomprehensible answer.

I tried a simpler approach.

"Why will it help, taking it to the West? Won't Western Intelligence feel the same way about it?"

"They do already." Again there was the grim chuckle. "In fact, it was Western Intelligence which first found out about it."

Worse and worse, this beating of my limited brains against a wall of fog.

"Let me explain," said my father, smiling at my obvious bewilderment. "We had two batteries, one in the United States, one here in Russia. By a sad mischance, the Americans discovered enough of the potentialities and uses to which a battery can be put. We then took steps to negate the position by removing the American battery."

"Just what I said."

"Removing it, not by destroying it, but by sending it home."

Mention of 'home' began a different train of thought. According to popular human belief the 'home' of the Outlanders lay far out in the solar system, beyond the planet Mars. I was on the point of asking my father whether this was so when with a gesture he indicated that I should remain silent.

"It was at this point that a complex game of psychological manoeuvre was started. Our disadvantage in this game lay in our lack of numbers. Very few of us were in concealed positions. You and I, Peter, but not many others."

"Why concealed positions?"

"For just such an emergency. But we had one big advantage. The Americans did not know we knew of their discovery. So the first move in the game lay with us."

"When you sent the thing home, weren't the Americans suspicious?"

My father smiled. "The human intelligence prides itself on its cleverness. Yet a psychology game is one that I too like to play. What were the Americans to think when we told them the battery had been sent home because of a serious flaw?"

"They'd be as suspicious as hell. I'd be suspicious as hell. The little old lady at the bottom of the street would be as suspicious as hell."

"Ah yes, but at the same time we asked for their cooperation, to assist us in the transport of *this* battery from out of Russia. *Now* what would you think?"

As my father spoke he patted the strange iridescent object with its curious shape.

"I suppose I'd play along," I answered.

"You wouldn't pass information to the East?"

"No, I wouldn't."

"Then, Peter my boy, you would have lost the first stage of this little game of ours."

My father now had a happy look about him.

"So for a while you would play along," he went on. "You would agree to introduce our agent into Russia, and you would also agree to arrange an exit route for him. And you would do all this slyly, so as not to excite Russian suspicions."

"O.K. That's what I would do."

"You would set your own agents to work, like the professor of Slavonic studies, and like Professor Ortov," said my father, grinning.

"I'd have appreciated it if you'd told me all this before," I muttered.

"That would not have been wise. It would have made it much harder for you to act the part of a simple student."

"I sure played it simple," I muttered again, trying to hide my chagrin.

Once again my father patted the battery thing.

"From the beginning, here in Russia, it had been necessary to go to ground with this. Because the Americans might have told the Russians about it."

"Not very likely, I'd say. But it would sure have been awkward if they had," I agreed.

"So awkward that it could not be permitted to happen," said my father, holding up a hand. "The worst thing for us would have been for the two political blocs to put their heads together in secret. We were therefore forced to take steps to negate that possibility."

"How could you stop it?"

"Very simply. Once the battery was safely to ground, we deliberately let the Russians discover its uses. This was certainly a material disadvantage to us, but it was an important psychological advantage, because now it was easy to deduce what the Russians would do."

"I can imagine."

"We not only permitted the Russians to discover something of the nature of the battery itself, but it was also arranged for them to learn of our joint plan with the Americans, which of course was a plan we did not intend to follow."

"So how would that set the Russians on a wrong track?"

"The Russians learned," my father went on relentlessly, "that at a certain time on a certain day there would be a meeting between an Outlander and an American agent."

"In the University bookstore?" I asked, part in irritation, part in amazement at this seeming insanity.

"Yes, in the bookstore. The place was carefully arranged. The two agents, the Russians learned, were to receive instructions contained within two similar books."

"Which had their ends cut away, I suppose," I continued in a sarcastic tone.

"Yes, that was it. And so, Peter, if you were in Russian shoes, what would you have done?"

"Somehow, I'd have found out what was in those books."

"And then?"

"I'd wait for the two agents to show up."

"And then?"

I thought for a while. "Well, then I'd wait around for them to make a move."

"Which your fellow agent, a man with an English voice, I believe, would certainly do. He would follow Western Intelligence's plan, and the Russians would keep close to him, carefully closing in, very gently."

My father's voice had a cheerfulness about it bordering on complacency.

"And what of me, might I ask?"

"Well, the Russians are thinking you also have been given instructions from the same Western plan. They have examined the cut-away book you were supposed to receive in the bookstore, and so they think they know all about you. But, because you were actually given only a normal copy of the book, you behave very differently from what the Russians expect. Instead of moving furtively, like the man with the English voice, you walk about quite openly, even carrying your copy of the book in clear public view. This is mysterious and puzzling. So you are permitted to go on walking about in your confident and easy style."

"To the Museum, I suppose?"

"Ah yes, but after you recognised the girl in the bookstore it was inevitable that your instinct would guide you to the Museum."

"Thank you," I said with as much dignity as I could muster.

"To that point you were entirely safe. You had no instructions. You had no idea of who you really were. The Russians would have had nothing of any importance against you, even if they'd picked you up."

"But after the Museum they would have had something." I remembered the curious inner flutter I'd felt when I left the Museum.

"They would have found you with travel documents to Armenia. Nothing more. Why shouldn't you go to Armenia?"

"Weren't you taking a risk of my being followed on the train?"

"A little. But we did something about that. Did you notice the poor lighting in the railway terminus? For an hour before your train was due to leave, we arranged to dip the supply on the power beams. In any case we had someone on the train, just to make sure."

"And if your someone on the train had suspected something?"

"Then we had alternate plans. We would have used a different scheme. You have the picture clear now?"

I thought for a while, and then said slowly, "So it all really turned on my being given a normal, ordinary copy of the Kransky book, when the Russians thought I was getting something else?"

My father chuckled again. "Delicate, wasn't it? Just one small move, using just one agent. Didn't I tell you that I enjoy these psychology games?"

I thought for a while, and then said, "I have the picture, except that I don't know how you are to go back and how I am to go forward from this place."

"Your way lies across the pass. At the far side you will be met."

"Who is to meet me?"

"You will be in no difficulty to recognize him."

"And you?"

"My way is already prepared."

"And if anything should go wrong?"

My father hesitated, obviously unwilling to admit that any plan of his might go wrong. At last he said grudgingly, "Should you need help, you must go to the Turkish city of Ankara, and there you must seek out a man known by the name of Dolfuss."

"Not much to go on."

"It will be enough."

It seemed that my father was unwilling to give me details of any part of the plan he felt it was unnecessary for me to know—which I suppose is a good basic rule of intelligence work.

In a general way I knew, as everybody else did, that the Outlanders had a space station at some place up on the Anatolian heights of Turkey. It had been chosen there to be tolerably balanced between Western and Eastern interests—in the West certainly, but farther in distance from the United States than from Russia. The 'battery,' as my father insisted on calling it, would be taken there by my contact. From the space station it would be despatched 'home.' Then, presumably, the human Earth people would once again fall under the control of the Outlanders.

Yet, with all this said, I still couldn't understand why my father and his fellow Outlanders had been foolish enough to bring these damn battery things to the Earth at all. By doing so they'd only piled up a lot of trouble for themselves. I was on the point of saying so when I fell asleep, as if a switch in my consciousness had suddenly been turned off.

No time at all later, it felt, my father was shaking me into wakefulness.

"Peter, it is two hours to dawn," he said. This was earlier than usual and I grunted in protest. "Today is not to be usual," he went on. "Today your way is to be prepared."

A soft radiance from the battery thing suffused the camp as I dressed. There was no heat to it, only light.

"I'd douse that light, Pop. It may give us away," I remonstrated.

For answer, my father did something that, so far from dousing the light, made it stronger. I finished dressing, hoping he knew what he was doing. It was still nowhere near dawn when my father told me to clip on my skis.

"You are to cross the plateau, back to the top of the same incline by which we came up to this place," he told me. "There you will wait, no matter what may befall, until the precise moment of dawn. Then, no matter what may have happened, you will return here to retrieve the battery. After that, be on your way up to the pass."

"I can't cross the plateau in the dark."

"A light will be made for you."

Even as he spoke, the light about the camp became brighter still.

"You're crazy," I protested. "They can't fail to see us."

As if he were indeed a priest of the Orthodox Church, my father lifted his arms high, his figure darkly silhouetted against the light behind.

"One last word," he cried. "Remember that no human must take this thing from you."

After this pronouncement there seemed little I could do, except move away. I knew nothing of the operation of the battery; otherwise I might have turned down the light, and told my father not to be such a confounded ass. As I poled away from the camp, I kept telling myself that somehow I should be taking charge of the position. The light was now so brilliant that it must have been visible for tens of kilometres around. Without difficulty, I could see our ski tracks of yesterday as they crossed the plateau.

I reached the place where yesterday the patrol of snow-cats had gone past, still with half an hour to go before dawn. The whole plateau glowed everywhere with the iridescent radiation.

The first grey light on the eastern horizon brought the helicopters. Even before that, I could hear the whine and buzz of many vehicles, and I could see the many red flares they were using to approach the plateau. As a pack of hounds closes for the kill, they swarmed to where my father and his damned battery were placed. I saw no sense in it, particularly no sense when the explosion came. There was no sudden pulse of sound or thunder clap. The light just went on and on growing brighter and brighter, and everywhere through the air there was a mighty ripping sound, as if giant sheets of calico were being torn into millions of pieces. Brighter and ever brighter. Although bright light cannot alone hurt your eyes, I was afraid of damaging ultraviolet, so I turned away from the thing. I think this may have been unnecessary, for my father had never warned me against it, and this light was the same as it had always been. Yet the scene before me was overwhelmingly intimidating.

As if by command, it was suddenly all gone. The world around me seemed dark, as if we had returned miraculously to the predawn hour. It was then that the thunder came. Peal after peal of it, roar upon roar. This I knew to be the sound of many avalanches on the surrounding slopes, where the snow had everywhere been subject to a sudden melting. Yet the snow around me was still firm and dry.

Gradually my eyes became accommodated to the normal light of day. Except where I was standing, the plateau had become a maze of pools, streams, and soft snow. In the direction of our former camp, the ground was bare. In moving away from the dry snow I cut quickly through the slush, wondering if the whole plateau had become intensely radioactive. But my father had told me to return, which he would not have done if there was radioactivity. The Russians would think of a nuclear explosion. They would expect radioactivity and would keep away for a while. I began to understand what my father had meant by saying he would prepare the way for me.

I soon came on to bare rock, and then had to carry my skis. The slope was gently downhill into a shallow bowl, about two kilometres in diameter. The rock was smooth, without boulders. At last it dawned on my numbed brain that this bowl must be new. It had been scored in some way in the rock by the explosion, an explosion so controlled that it had somehow left intact my position at the far side of the plateau, even to the extent of not melting the snow over there.

It was absurd to expect my father to be still in that fiercely scored pit. Nor was he, although in my bemused state I looked everywhere for his body. Nor were burned-out wrecks of helicopters or snowcats anywhere to be seen. The blasting of a two-kilometre crater could have left nothing of human manufacture. It had not.

Yet at the bottom of this crater I found the battery thing. It lay there, its shape unchanged. The curious pattern of light still played on its surface, the pattern which, with averted consciousness, I seemed in some way to understand.

To make room for this 'battery,' a ridiculous name for an object of such furious power, I discarded everything except my thermal bag and a three-day ration of food from my pack. To my further surprise the thing had already become quite cool, so I had no difficulty in lifting it up and stowing it away. Then with my skis over my shoulder I walked slowly, and in great sadness, up and out of the bowl.

A steep wall of rock and ice on the right side of the pass dropped in a huge cascade from a peak, marked on the map as the Ogre. This imposing sight was contrasted by a more gently rising snowfield to the left. A quick look at the place and I knew I didn't like it. The pass itself was perhaps a hundred yards wide. I had approached it up a snow-filled couloir exposed to avalanches from the Ogre. To avoid this danger, it was tempting to move out to the left, but I knew the criss-crossed irregularities in the snow out there were hidden crevasses, under no circumstances to be attempted by a lone man.

I moved on cautiously until I could see something of the western side of the pass, which I liked even less. Standing on the head of the pass now, my lungs working like the bellows of an old-fashioned steel mill, I gazed down into the gloom. It was early in the day, the second day since the incidents on the snow plateau, so the Sun still hadn't reached the deep trench ahead of me. The vast gorge I looked down dropped away according to my map for some five thousand feet. In one swooping glide the snow fell steeply for perhaps fifteen hundred feet. Then it disappeared over a great precipice, where I could see spires of black rock sticking out of the slope. Above those spires ran a slanting traverse opening up towards the right. I wondered if this could be the traverse mentioned by the man from the Museum. From above, it looked only an apology of a thing, but there seemed to be no other.

I plotted my route down the slope. Just keep an iron control on yourself over the first five hundred feet, then slow down and keep slowing until the exit traverse to the right shows itself. If need be I'd stop, and edge my way over to the right. Easy enough in words, but there was a big trouble to it, and that trouble was the snow. It was badly waterlogged. Below the white surface, snow was melting even this early in the morning. The perfect condition for an avalanche. The more I looked at the slope the more I knew the damned thing would slide away from me as soon as I touched it. I could see myself contained in a boiling flurry, sliding inevitably towards those black rock spires. Then down and down, spectacularly down, over the precipice, into the valley below. "From the fat into the fire," I muttered to myself.

Filling my lungs with cold, damp air, I pushed myself

outward, jumping to avoid a small crevasse that appeared in front of me as I picked up speed. In spite of the poor light of the early morning my eyes had not deceived me. It was steep, very steep indeed, down this western side of the pass. My father had been right. He could not have followed me here.

A number of times before in my life I'd been in minor avalanches, and close to some big ones too. An avalanche starts with a spray of small snowflakes, which appear deceitfully harmless. A few members of this first cloud of white particles continue their downward journey, growing as they fall. Then quite suddenly these particles become larger aggregates of snow, pieces the size of footballs.

It takes a little while for these first signs of the avalanche to appear, so your natural instinct is to swoop rapidly downwards, congratulating yourself that you've kept well ahead of any trouble. But once the slope behind really peels away, it sweeps downwards to the depths below at a speed you cannot match. A wall of snow races downhill faster than an express train. In a flash you vanish within it, legs, arms, and skis, quite out of control. Then you're simply carried along by the momentum of the avalanche. On this slope I would be carried towards the black spires, a momentary prelude to the final plunge down more than three thousand feet of almost vertical ice-caked rock.

Even as I watched the ground slipping ever faster away beneath me, I saw the first small millimetre-sized particles of snow fly away into the air, the apparently insubstantial harbingers of disaster, and I knew I had to restrain the well-nigh overwhelming impulse to race ahead. I had to do exactly the opposite. By a fierce series of turns across the slope I kept as high as I could. I had to allow the snow to overtake me as soon as possible, before its downward momentum became quite irresistible.

As the spray swirled about my head, visibility became essentially nil. Such control as I had came from my thighs. The tension in my leg muscles was now my sole contact with the hostile environment around me. Then inevitably I was fighting to keep my head above a falling wall of snow. My mind was equally overwhelmed by the thought that my pack would be torn loose from my back, to be swept over the precipice below. And so it would all have been for nothing, nothing at all.

My slide gradually slowed. For a brief moment I had the luxury of congratulating myself that I'd completed the most difficult of all skiing manoeuvres, deliberately starting an avalanche and then avoiding its consequences. This exuberance was soon quelled, as the weight of snow began to compact about my chest. Inexorably, implacably, the pressure increased, until collapsed ribs and punctured lungs seemed inevitable.

The suffocating world of strangulation came to a stop. Blindly I fought to free myself. I clawed to reach the light with the determination of the insane. I dug towards it furiously, winning a small release from the forces which bound my chest in a steel-tight girdle. The first slight victory was fully as difficult as all the rest. I fought the horrible wet snow like a drowning cat. Lionlike, prehensile, I fought to the surface of the snow, where at last I could breathe air into my aching lungs, air instead of ice crystals. I lay there a long time recovering.

My first thought was that the pack was still safe. Indestructible, my father had said. But my skis were gone. Without them the mountainside seemed vast, immense, beyond the reach of any skill. Then I saw the tip of a ski. I moved slowly towards it, testing the thick band of snow debris around me with infinite care, for I feared that it might start to move again.

I retrieved the one ski and reset the binding on my boot. One ski and no sticks was not a promising combination, but it was better than it might have been. Then I moved downward through soft slushy rubbish for some hundred and fifty feet, listening intently for any slight sound that might presage a new slippage of the snow around me. Eventually I reached a steep hard surface, a black nightmare for the prepared-slope skier.

The ice below me, stripped by the avalanche of its snow covering, glistened with an evil challenge. With two skis and sticks I could have moved down with care, relying on the steel edges of my skis to give me the slight purchase I needed. But with one ski and only a pair of arms, I had no choice except to take the slope in bow-shaped traverses, slightly downhill but mostly sideways. Once I picked up any speed at all, I cut hard into the icy surface, so as to move into an uphill line, eventually slowing to a stop. Then with great effort I made an awkward stationary turn and so began the manoeuvre again.

To my astonishment and frank disbelief, I suddenly saw my second ski, perhaps three hundred feet below. Hardly crediting that comparative safety might be so close, I shortened my traverses of the slope. The nearer I came to the ski, the more care I took. Gremlins, gremlins, I kept muttering to myself.

After breaking loose, the ski had gone sliding at first, then jumping and leaping on its way to the depths below. Somewhere on its journey, however, it had taken an extra large leap which had brought it almost precisely at a vertical angle into the slope. The speed and the sharp point had caused it to dig into the hard surface and it had remained there as the avalanche swept downwards. It remained there, a mute testimony to the laws of chance.

I was within a couple of yards of retrieving the ski when I realised things weren't well, for nothing was left of the binding. I gave the metal ski a tug and it came clear, minus its head. I was tempted to reset it, sprouting there from the ice, but then I realised it would only remain as a signpost for any others who might be following behind me. So I laid the damaged ski on the slope and watched as it accelerated down to the black spires of rock, now perhaps five hundred feet below me. In one majestic leap out into space it was gone. Carefully I turned, slowly crossing and recrossing the ice, until after an eternity the snow traverse down to the right opened up.

As I reached its shelter, I realised that my chest was hurting horribly. I spat into the snow, expecting to see blood in the spittle. The way I felt there should have been blood, but with wearisome relief I saw there was none. At least my lungs were not punctured.

The traverse led down and ever downwards. With normal equipment I would have made short work of it, but with only the one ski I was reduced to a slow crawl. For a while I could see a lake in the distance, which I thought must be Cala. Then as I lost height it disappeared behind an intervening range of mountains.

There was an obvious long tongue of snow which avoided a series of crevasses on the glacier below. It also led past a sequence of tedious moraines at the side of the glacier, degenerating at last into bare ground. From there, within an hour, I reached a stony track that wound its way tortuously among the lower moraines, down to which the glacier must have reached in ages past. There seemed little point in continuing to carry my solitary ski, so I found a cleft between large boulders and threw it down in there, well out of sight of anyone walking the track.

Some while later, my eye caught the distant outline of a hut, projected against a barren stony background. In a numb state of mind I set myself to grind out the further kilometre or two that would be needed to reach it. The hut was sure to have liquid, and it was liquid that I craved, for I had had none since quitting the melted snow plateau two days before.

I had taken the battery thing out of my pack when I stopped on the evening of the first of the two days, thinking I might use it to melt snow, as my father had done. There was the same iridescence about it as there always had been. But of external controls, switches, or anything like that there were none. It was that same curiously shaped, strangely patterned thing, apparently entirely enclosed in itself. With the thought that either my father, or the explosion which he had initiated, must have stripped away the controls, I had replaced it in my pack, and had resigned myself to going waterless for the rest of the journey.

The hut was no different from a thousand and one other mountain huts of its type. It had a lower storey with a wood stove, a long table, and wooden benches, and an upper storey with several bunks on which were small heaps of slightly damp, slightly musty, blankets. There were the usual three or four wooden steps leading up to the outer door, on which your boots made the dull sounds which signal the end, or the beginning, of the active part of a mountaineering day. And there was the usual store of chopped wood and the box of large old-fashioned red phosphorus-tipped matches, worrisomely damp, but which eventually splutter into flame, so long as you are careful not to strip them by a too vigorous rubbing.

I longed for tea, but there was none in my pack. Nor was any tea to be found in the hut. So I had perforce to be content with a first drink of cold water from a metal tank outside the hut. Then I prepared a squelchy mass of one of the dehydrated foods. I ate two large bowlfuls of the stuff, and at the same time toasted my legs, which ached unconscionably from the slow and strenuous descent, in front of the stove.

It was just as I finished the second bowl that I heard the heavy footsteps. Outside, at first over the gritty rock, and then the clump clump clump on the wooden steps. The door creaked as it opened.

My father had said I would know the man who would come to meet me. He had not been wrong.

It was a diminutive round-faced figure, with pince-nez stuck on the end of a sharp nose, who stood there in the doorway of the hut. Instead of a windcheater, he now wore a bulging fur jacket, which made him seem almost as broad as he was long. The strain of my descent from the pass, contrasting ludicrously with memories of the wallowings of the Sno' Skeeter from Maryland, made me bark out in a shrill laugh.

"The name is Edelstam. I don't suppose you remembered it," he said, as he put down with obvious relief the pack he had been carrying.

"I beg your pardon, Mr. Edelstam," I replied, still unable to wipe the grin off my face.

"How was the descent from the pass?"

"Difficult."

"I always said it would be. Too difficult. But at least it avoided suspicion. And you're safe and well, which is the main thing. I brought you some tea. I thought you might like it."

Edelstam took a bag from his jacket pocket, and then looked around with a gathering frown.

"You brought the pack?" he asked sharply.

"Upstairs."

He made no answer, but thumped his way up the single steep wooden stairs which linked the lower and upper areas of the hut. I could hear him thudding around above my head as I set about heating water for the tea. I reckoned I could happily drink a gallon of it, just in my first cup, except there were no mugs of that size among the limited crockery to be found in the storage cupboard of the hut.

Edelstam made his way back down the wooden stairs, as always making quite a noise about it.

"Good, I see you brought it. Congratulations."

It may seem strange, and it was strange, that I should have allowed Edelstam, on only our very brief former acquaintance, to go upstairs and to search the pack which I had been at such literal pains to bring across the well-nigh impossible barrier of the pass, a pack which I knew to contain an object that could scour a two-kilometre-diameter crater from out of solid rock. The reason too was strange.

I had felt a strong sense of responsibility for it from the moment I'd set out two days before from the snow plateau. Quite abnormally strong in fact, so strong as to impel me to attempt the descent from the pass, something that, crazy as I had always been in such things, I would normally have hesitated to do. Yet from the moment Edelstam appeared at the hut door this strong sense of responsibility disappeared. It was clean gone now. I felt I couldn't care less about the damn battery. And my father had simply said I would know the man who would come to me. How else would I know him except in this instinctive kind of way?

Even so, there were still matters I was curious about. With a mug of steaming tea in one hand, I took Edelstam's shoulder with the other, and then led him outside the hut. Although I'm pretty big, husky my father had said, I made little sound on the wooden steps compared to Edelstam's strange tramp. I couldn't figure how he did it, unless he was wearing lead plates in his boots. Another thing I couldn't figure out was how such an ungainly fellow had gotten himself to this place. Although the hut was perhaps four thousand feet below the pass, it was still well up in the mountains, as was indeed obvious from the wild landscape around us. True the track must lead down to the lower valley, but such a clumsy fellow as this Edelstam would be out of place even on the simplest path anywhere among high mountains.

"How did you get here?" I asked.

"I'd rather not answer that question if you don't mind" was the calm reply.

"Why not?"

"For the good reason that you can never be made to tell what you don't know, can you?"

"I'm not going to tell anybody anything."

"It's hard to be sure, isn't it? There are people in this world who are specialists in making other people tell the things they don't want to tell. Look, Peter—may I call you Peter?—the position is still very complex, very complex

47

indeed. We have done well so far, but there is still a long long way to go."

"I hope you know what's to be done next."

"It is complex," the little man repeated, "complex, like a problem in physics. You know, I once won a Nobel Prize for physics. I find it very odd to be in a place like this, and in a situation like this."

Mention of physics, and his oblique reference to the torture squads of the intelligence agencies, immediately raised doubts in my mind. As if he read it in my face, Edelstam launched himself into an account of events of my boyhood, in the days of my cross-country trips with my father.

"There, you see," he concluded, "you are not to worry yourself about me."

"How is your daughter?" I asked, with real concern.

"Alive and well. You are not to worry about her either," he replied.

"Suppose you tell me just what's worrying *you*," I came back.

"Well, let's start with the explosion, the one you saw two days ago."

"I can't understand it," I said. "That damned explosion openly advertised our position." I stood there, scratching my head with one hand and holding a still half-filled mug of tea with the other.

"As well as being an explosion, there was a transmission of information, which it was critical to send at that time, a transmission of information far out into space."

"What information?"

"Once again, it would be better for you not to know."

"O.K. I'm not to know. But the explosion sure advertised our position."

48

"Not too seriously, I would say. Perhaps you know of the Outlanders' space station in Anatolia? Well, it was obvious, wasn't it, that an attempt would be made to cross the frontier into Turkey?"

"O.K. But it wasn't obvious whereabouts on the frontier, not until after the explosion."

"True, but the place of the explosion instantly became the precise spot where, because of fear of radioactivity, neither the Americans nor the Russians would dare to look closely, at any rate for a few hours, until their detectors had shown them there was no radioactivity. By then you were away from the place, en route for the pass."

"I certainly wasn't worried by helicopters, I'll agree to that. But if they had spotted me, it would have been easy for them to close off the pass. There was a two-hundred-yard gap up there for them to land in."

"Think, Peter, think! Try putting yourself in *their* shoes, not always in your own."

"How come?"

"Look, they find a whacking great crater at this place. Who thinks anybody could have escaped from an explosion like that? Who thinks anybody could cross the frontier over a pass like that? What they're thinking is that this God-damned battery has gone up in smoke, along with all the rock and snow. And that, Peter, has got everybody badly worried, because now the Outlanders can clip the wings of world governments by cutting the power beams. So it's all polite diplomacy, and hugs and kisses, and let's-be-friends again."

"So why are you worried, Mr. Edelstam?"

"Because behind all the smiles-from-the-teeth-outward, they're going to keep a damn close watch on everything going into that space station."

49

"I see. So it's your job to get this battery thing in there."

Embarrassment shone on Edelstam's face. He indicated that we return to the hut, which I was nothing loath to do, for I had a mind to drink much more of the tea. I set myself to make no sound on the wooden steps. Edelstam gave not the slightest notice to my catlike antics, half deafened, no doubt, by his own monstrous tread.

We sat on opposite sides of the long wooden table. While I poured the tea, Edelstam fiddled with his fingers.

"My real problem," he said at last, "is to know what to do with you, Peter."

"I guess I can look after myself."

"Ridiculous. Both the Americans and the Russians know about you, about your connexion with this business. The moment you show your face in public they'll be all over you."

"Well, I won't have the battery, will I? So why should I worry?"

"I think you would find the experience most unpleasant."

I began to see now what Edelstam was driving at. There were many things I didn't know, most things in fact, but at least I knew about the battery. I knew it still existed. In the circumstances, a most important piece of information.

"Then I'd better go to ground, until you have it safely into space," I said, indicating the pack upstairs by a lift of my mug.

Edelstam's embarrassment increased, to a point where I began to wonder if he was going to say it would be better still for me to return over the pass, and then to fall into a crevasse or something.

"So I had hoped," he said at length, "and if the Americans and Russians had gone on opposing each other, it would have been easily possible to play it like that."

"Sure they oppose each other, the way a dog opposes a cat."

"I've known a dog and a cat who didn't fight with each other, improbable as it may seem," said Edelstam, smiling, "and improbable as it may seem, the Americans and Russians have done a lot of talking during the past two days. You see, they were both deceived, which gives them common ground. Diplomatically speaking, they're both in the same difficulty. If anything should turn up, if you should turn up, or I should turn up, they've the same common interest in seizing what must seem to be a kind of last chance."

I could see this clearly enough, and I could see Edelstam was going to have his work cut out in getting my pack through to the space station. When I said so, he nodded vigorously, as if to indicate that I'd relieved him of a difficulty.

"Yes," he said, still nodding, so that I thought the pince-nez must soon fall from his nose. "You see, Peter, it does not help a great deal any longer that the battery is believed at the diplomatic level not to exist. The intelligence agencies will still be given instructions to go on searching for it, on the assumption that it exists."

"I guess it costs them nothing," I agreed.

"So we have to ask ourselves," continued Edelstam, "if we are really gaining very much from holding back."

"Holding back on what?"

"On the existence of the battery."

"How could their knowing it help us?"

"It would if they thought the battery to be somewhere else, in the city of Ankara, shall we say."

"How would they come to think that?" I kept asking.

"The simplest plan would be for you, Peter, to make your way, somewhat openly, to Ankara."

"I see," I said slowly, drinking the last of the tea. "You want me to take the heat off."

"It is for you to decide. I can only ask."

"Give me a few moments," I grunted, rising from the table, and making my way outside again, alone. There were heavy clouds down now on the mountains above the hut. I looked up, glad not to be still struggling with the ice slope and with the precipice below. There was a distant rumble, an avalanche. In these conditions there would be many of them. I was aware now how much my life had changed in the past weeks. From the time of my visit to the Museum everything was different. No return to my student life. No return to Ketchum, Idaho. So what was there for me to do now? Where should I go? First to Ankara, and then perhaps to the 'home' of the Outlanders? This would at least be a sensible possibility. I would at least learn a little about the things which remained unclear in my mind, the veritable valley of darkness I perceived to be deep inside me. So I returned inside to Edelstam and told him that I agreed to do what he wanted of me.

For answer, he immediately went to the pack he had deposited when he first entered the hut. From it he drew out an object of about the same size as the battery thing. It had no curiosity of shape, being simply a burnished metal box. Nor was there any iridescence about it.

"It is not quite without virtue," said Edelstam, as if he read my thoughts.

"Virtue?"

"Anyone seeking to open it up will be in for a big surprise," he replied, grinning. I followed his finger to a join in the metal.

"But it's no battery?"

Edelstam chuckled and shook his head.

"I suppose you couldn't tell me the difference?"

"I can tell you a bit about the battery itself, if you're really interested."

"I'd have thought that would be another of the things it wouldn't be wise for me to know," I said sarcastically. Edelstam showed no concern. "What I can tell you about it would not be of much use in itself, not without having the thing itself," he continued.

"O.K. I'm listening."

"Start with an ordinary battery. When a conductor, a piece of metal or something like that, is put across the terminals of a battery, an electric current flows in the conductor. O.K.?"

"O.K.," I agreed.

"Why?"

"Search me."

"Because of something called an electromotive force, an EMF as it's usually called."

"I've heard of that."

"But you don't know what causes it?"

"No."

"Well, it comes basically from chemical changes within the battery, from atoms changing the way they fit themselves into molecules. O.K.?"

"I'm with you, more or less."

"Now you might think of playing something like the same trick, not with molecules, which only involve the outer electronic parts of atoms, but with the inner nuclear parts. If you could do that, you might expect your battery to become about a million times more powerful than an ordinary battery. But you can't. At least no one has yet been able to do so. You still with me?"

"You'd have something a bit like a nuclear explosion?"

"Sort of."

"But that thing," I said, pointing upstairs, "seems to me to be quite a bit more powerful than a nuclear explosion."

"Well, you must understand the particles which make up the nucleus of an ordinary atom are themselves made up of other particles, and these other particles are themselves made up of a still finer-scale structure. And perhaps there are even more details, which neither I nor anybody else knows anything about. Normally, these inner features never change, which is good for us, because fantastic energies would be involved. To give you an idea, imagine a tiny piece of matter, so small that you could just see it in a microscope. Well, any energetic reshuffling of this innermost kind, affecting even such a microscopic piece, would be as powerful as an H-bomb. O.K.?"

"You're telling me something of that sort goes on in this battery thing?"

"Right, Peter, right! Except in some way that is quite beyond my power of comprehension it is all carefully controlled. It's not just a matter of a random explosion. In fact, it *is* like an ordinary battery. It can be switched on and off, and it can be directed in its use. How the devil that's done I don't know. Maybe one day I'll find out."

Thinking that my father must have understood the operation of the battery, I lapsed into a reverie. After giving me a moment or two, Edelstam took me by the arm,

"But that's enough physics," he said, "let's be a bit clearer in our plans. You are going to give me twelve hours before you leave this place." At this, Edelstam took a small box from a pocket of his fur jacket. "Sleeping pill," he continued. "Use it, otherwise you'll be restless with exhaustion. After you're refreshed, take my pack and simply go on from here as best you can. Keep them off my back for four or five days—say, for a week. In that time you'll not expect any help from us. O.K.?"

"Help?" I asked.

"At the end of a week we'll take steps to pick you up."

"Fine. I'll try not to need any help."

Edelstam nodded, somewhat gravely. "I'm sure you won't," he agreed.

"Besides, if I need help I know what to do," I added.

"Peter, I'm sure you're very resourceful. So perhaps you'd help me down with the pack upstairs."

I fetched the pack and adjusted the straps to fit Edelstam's smaller height. Then with a nod he took my hand.

"And the best of luck. Thanks," he said.

"The best to you."

Then he was gone, his tread on the wooden hut steps just as heavy as before. I resisted the temptation to follow him outside. Somewhere among the moraines I felt there had to be a waiting helicopter, since Edelstam was too slight a man to carry his heavy load for more than an odd kilometre or two. The clouds which had gathered would provide him with good cover. But this was not my concern or responsibility.

I took Edelstam's pack upstairs with me. After shaking out several of the blankets, and then making a satisfactory nest in one of the bunks, I opened the small box he had given me. I became unconscious in a fraction of a second. The last I remember was a sudden fizz from the box, not unlike the sound of an aerosol can.

I must have been flat out through just about twelve hours, for it was in the early hours of the following morning that I awoke. I stumbled in the darkness, finding my way down the wooden flight of stairs to the lower storey. Then I began a bruising search for the box of phosphorus-tipped matches. During this somewhat lengthy process I felt quite as clumsy as Edelstam had sounded, but at last I had the matches, and from them a glimmer of light. Instantly I could move about with ease.

With the wood stove going, and with the blood circulating again in my limbs, I gave further thought to Mr. Edelstam. He'd certainly made sure of my not leaving the hut for the twelve hours he needed. After rummaging in my bunk, I found the box which was supposed to contain the 'sleeping pill.' As I had deduced, it in fact contained a small cylinder, with a valve that opened with the lid of the box. It had obviously contained some kind of knockout gas, mixed under pressure with a neutral gas like freon. Opening the box had thrown a cloud of the stuff about my face.

As I sipped the further tea which I made, I reflected on Edelstam's description of those boyhood events, events he could only have learned about from my father. Reluctantly, for I was mad about the box, I decided he must be O.K. Maybe the idea had been just to warn me against my own cockiness, just as his showing me the picture of his supposed daughter had given a useful warning in the Moscow University bookstore. While turning these thoughts over in my mind, I managed to stuff more of the food, after watering and heating it, into my belly—no easy task at this hour of the morning.

I waited until the first glimpse of dawn. Then I swung

Edelstam's pack on to my back and began my descent down the stony track from the hut. In the faint light it hadn't been possible to tidy away the obvious signs of my visit there, as a mountaineer is always supposed to do. But Edelstam had asked me to travel openly. So why not begin traveling openly right away?

This was the only refreshing thought of a long and miserable day, for the way led down into one of those long, barren, uninhabited valleys which seem to have missed out on every redeeming feature. The track wound its way, with infuriating detours, first along one side of a brawling boulder-strewn stream, then along the other. At each turn of the valley I hoped for a change, for the first signs of pasturage. But throughout the day, I was disappointed. Darkness found me beside a rough stone wall, however. I built shelter from the wind from a bit of the wall and from other stones which lay to hand. Cursing myself for letting Edelstam go off with my thermal bag, I settled down to a long chilly night of it.

I stamped about a good deal the following morning, returning circulation to my extremities, getting the blood into my stiffened legs. It was still quite barren, with a few patches of grass dotted here and there among the outcrops of rock. The sky was blue and clear, with sunrise not far away. A few birds perched on a nearby section of the wall, twittering as if to afford me a modicum of companionship. I drank water from a stream, and then stirred some of it into a packet of food, achieving a sort of paste, which I ate as best I could.

As I set off once more along the bleak valley, a wave of nostalgia swept over me for my home in Idaho. As I gazed across this unattractive countryside, my thoughts turned to the Snake River, Hell's Canyon, and to the mountains,

Sawtooth and the Seven Devils. I wondered if I would ever see them all again. I'd left Idaho in high spirits, not dreaming of what the following months would have in store for me. I wondered about the future, which still lay like a dark patch in my mind, a patch in which I could see visions of many figures, of the Englishman and of the girl in the bookstore, of Edelstam and of my father. Certain it was that Edelstam had not walked this endless valley.

But end it did at last. I came by mid-morning to a well-used unsurfaced road, which continued down the main valley, always in a westerly direction. My boots crunched rhythmically in the dirt, the sound lulling me into further visions of Idaho, of its forests and rushing streams, of its farmlands and its sage-covered uplands.

I was startled by a noise from behind, nobody so far as I was aware being behind me. Yet glancing back I saw a small cart drawn by a mule. It was coming my way, and oddly enough it seemed to be empty. I waited until it came up alongside, and only then did I see a small girl standing behind the high wooden front of the cart.

"Good morning," I called.

The girl glanced at me with obvious suspicion, immediately flicking at the reins. The mule took no notice, however, plodding on exactly as before. I walked beside the cart for a while and tried again, this time in Russian. The girl now looked quite terrified, so I allowed the cart to pull slowly ahead of me, much as I would have appreciated a lift to relieve the tedium of this long trudge.

The Sun had risen toward its midday altitude. In the lower valley now, I became overhot in my fur suit. I stripped off the upper part of it, stuffing it into the top of the pack, above the boxlike metal object. There was nothing to be done about the fur trousers, so perforce I had to continue wearing them, conscious that I must look a distinctly peculiar object. Edelstam had asked me to move openly. I was sure open, as open as the Sun in the sky.

The road thereafter became paved. Perhaps two hours further on, I saw a truck some way ahead, parked by the roadside. My instinct told me to seek a wide detour, but true to the new doctrine of openness I kept to the road, albeit in a fair degree of wariness.

"Hello, stranger on the road," a voice called in a language not known to me, Turkish presumably.

"Hi," I replied, watching as a fellow with dark hair, moustache, and eyes scrambled out from the roadside ditch.

"You look tired," the man continued with a not particularly convincing smile.

I shrugged my shoulders to indicate that I didn't understand.

Without warning, I was suddenly grabbed by the arm and pushed toward three other men who had also risen from the ditch.

"Drink! Are you hungry?" I was asked.

A large tin mug was thrust into my hand and wine was slopped into it from a huge bottle. One of the men then handed me a hefty lump of cheese and a hunk of bread. These seemed friendly gestures, so I grinned and said, "Thanks, fellers."

As I ate and drank, the four babbled away in their own language—it's funny how any language you don't understand always sounds like that, a senseless babble. I peered into the ditch, where I could see lengths of piping and sundry tools scattered about. Workmen evidently. This relieved my mind, and I began to wonder about getting a lift from them at the end of the day.

When the meal was finished, the man who had been first out of the ditch indicated by signs that in one or two hours, it wasn't clear which, the party would be returning down the valley. For my part, I indicated that I would be glad to wait, and the man touched his moustache with an understanding wink.

I think I must have dozed a bit as I waited there. In spite of my enforced twelve hours back at the mountain hut, I still had a lot of catching up on sleep to do, especially after the stony billet of the preceding night. I awoke to find the men loading up the truck. I climbed in through the tailgate, together with my moustachioed friend and one of the others, the remaining two mounting into the driver's cab. With an incompetent grinding of gears we were off. I slipped the pack from my back, grinning as I did so, and then settled down to take the weight off my legs. I sat the way we were going, facing the other two, who had their backs against the cab. Before long they were nodding off to sleep, and for my part I tried to rest as best I could.

I remember the sensation of being lifted up. There was a wobbling, which in my sleep-drugged state I took to be the motion of the truck. Then my body hit something that knocked the wind out of me. I was not conscious of pain at this first impact, but the second one hurt badly. There was blood before my eyes as my face parted from the rock it had hit. A steel-hard surface ended my fall. I gulped for air and ice-cold water rushed into my mouth.

It was the chill of the water that saved me. The shock of it pulled me back from a grey and ghostly world, to find myself wedged between two large rocks in the bed of a mountain river. I shook my head, shipping more water, and looked up. Above me, I could see the road as it turned a corner, with a small bridge in the middle of the curve.

In a flash of regaining consciousness, I realised that I must have pitched out of the truck as it crossed the bridge. I'd hit the water, and then I'd bashed myself as the strong current carried me from rock to rock. It was then I noticed that only one eye was working. The other had the eyebrow pushed hard down into its socket, and the left side of my face had been severely pulped.

I was shivering badly now, both from shock and from the water. I struggled to pull myself free of the rocks, to unjam myself. As I came upright, I realised at last just how steep the stream bed really was. Not far below me, the cascade disappeared over a rocky lip. With my good eye I could see spray billowing upwards from falling water.

Even in retrospect, I do not care to remember the manner of my escape from that river. The only way out of it lay upwards, back up the cascade. I had to haul myself from one treacherous piece of rock to another, against the force of the current, until I could get a purchase on one of the rock walls which contained the course of the river. Only the desperation which comes with death a hair's-breadth away gave me the strength to climb that wall and so to regain the road.

My first thought was that the truck must have crashed at the bridge—I remembered how the incompetent driver had fouled the gears when we started. But there was no sign of an accident there, or of my pack. So the wine I had been given, with such a kindly flourish, had been spiced with some long-acting drug, and in my stupefied state I must have been thrown out of the truck by my erstwhile friends. It was absurd that I should have escaped through the fine net of Russian security only to fall for a simple trick like this. In my pain and anger I resolved, once I was in better command of myself, to make those four bastards pay heavily for it.

But this was not to be. I had not staggered an hour further along the road when I turned a corner to see a fire burning beneath a tree. It crackled in a welcoming fashion as I moved forward to reach its beckoning warmth. Then perhaps sixty yards beyond I saw the tailgate of the truck, with smoke curling above it. When I reached it, I found to my surprise only the rear end part. The front of the truck appeared simply to have disintegrated. I looked around for the men themselves. I found one, a blackened corpse, hanging from a blackened tree, and I found sufficient dismembered remains of the others to convince me that the debt had already been paid.

Something with the force of a landmine had evidently exploded. It was not difficult to connect the explosion with the metal box in Edelstam's pack, the pack which the four men had been at such pains to steal from me. I continued laboriously along the road. It was tempting to stay by the warm fire, but prudence suggested that I should seek to disconnect myself, if at all possible, from the gruesome scene beside the shattered truck. I remember reviewing these possibilities in my mind. A common robbery? A Western security operation, waiting there as I emerged from the crossing of the frontier? Or Edelstam seeking his diversion? I was on the point of making pain-wracked decisions on these questions when blackness overwhelmed me. To be plain, I lurched forward and pitched unconscious onto the roadway ahead.

I must have lain there in the road for many hours, until a passing vehicle noticed me, and until aid was summoned from a distant hospital. It is hardly to be believed that these passing hours were eventually to prove to my advantage, but they were steadily shortening the remaining part of the week's diversion I had promised to Edelstam. The next thing I remember was a sea of white faces looking down at me. I was about to try to sit up when I felt a hand on my shoulder. There was a faint prick in my arm, which I took to be a hypodermic needle. A voice swirled about my ears, saying, as I guessed afterwards, *"That should relieve some of the pain."* I grunted in English, "Thanks, brother."

In answer another voice asked, "You are English?"

"American," I managed to gasp out, before the numbing effect of the drug made everything dim and vague again. I sensed that I was being lifted. Then I heard a motor start up. It had a curious sound about it, since my brain accepted only the lower-pitched sounds—a strange, distant, echoing sound. Then the black ocean which perpetually surrounds our small island of consciousness swept over me once more.

I returned to my senses for the second time with an appalling dried-out sensation in my mouth, and with a far more precise appreciation of my surroundings.

"Where am I?" I asked in a frog-like croak.

A small dark-haired pretty girl looked down on me, a trolley beside her.

"Don't try to speak now," she said in English.

"Just tell me where I am. Then I'll shut up."

"In Erzurum. This is the Western Military Hospital."

Then I heard the trolley being wheeled away. I tried to open my damaged eye, but nothing happened. I moved a hand carefully towards it, and found it to be covered by an extensive bandage. I remembered that I had been able to climb and walk, so presumably the rest of me was in an unbroken condition. But, just to check, I stealthily moved my hands around, searching for bandages and splints. There was a bandage on one arm but fortunately no splints. Since I could move the arm, I felt the wound there could not be particularly serious. The problem came down then to my left eye and cheek, particularly to whether the sight in my eye would return. There was no way this could be decided for the moment, so I settled back on the bed to assess the situation.

Although my face was beginning already to itch madly —a sign of the quick healing I mentioned before—it was pleasant to enjoy the easing of the pain, so pleasant that it was tempting simply to go on lying there in the comparative comfort of the bed. As far as I could tell, I must have been brought into this particular hospital because I had told the ambulance crew I was American. This inevitably meant that enquiries would be made, at first in a general way and then with increasing momentum. Pretty soon I could be expecting a visit from Western Intelligence. This was on the assumption that my meeting with the Turkish workmen had not itself been an intelligence operation, a supposition which was more or less proved by subsequent events—indeed, by the fact that I was not being questioned right now. My feeling was that the affair of the truck and the stream, and of the landmine, had quite a different explanation, one I hoped to investigate at a future date.

The decision now to be made was whether I should go on lying there, a sitting duck for the intelligence men. I saw three reasons why I shouldn't. The first was simply that I had no liking for being a sitting duck. The second was that I wouldn't be able to create a very credible diversion. The explosion which had wrecked the truck might look like the work of the battery thing—I was sure this had been Edelstam's intention—but since the remains of the battery thing were not to be found at the site of the explosion itself, and since I didn't have it myself, it would be clear that it should be sought elsewhere—at the Anatolian space station, for example—which was just the wrong thing to happen. The right thing was for Western Intelligence to believe that I was still connected with the damn thing, and this meant that I must be up and away from my bed just as soon as I possibly could.

My third reason for wanting to move was a personal one. I was in Erzurum now, whereas I had said I would make my way to Ankara. It wasn't that I cared so much about my promise to Edelstam. But what I had set myself to do I wanted to do. I didn't have too many clear objectives in life by now, but this at least was one of them. So goodbye to my rest, goodbye to my bed, goodbye to the pretty dark-haired nurse with the trolley.

In the making of this decision, I set a lot on my past experience with injuries, and on the itching of my face, which would soon be driving me crazy. It felt as if a thousand mosquitoes were biting away at me.

I waited until a nurse, not the one with the trolley, poked into my room—this kind of momentary entrance and exit seems to occur in all hospitals all the time. I asked her for directions to the toilet.

"Are you sure you're all right?" she asked.

"Of course. No broken bones, just a bash on my face. That's all," I assured her.

She looked at a chart attached to the bottom of the bed.

"You really shouldn't be walking around. Not yet," she went on with a frown.

"It'll make it easier," I said, hauling myself up off the bed.

In the end she let me go, as I knew she would. My skiing injuries had led me to spend a few days in hospital on quite a number of occasions. So I knew that the nursing staff are only too glad when a patient can attend to his own elementary needs. There would be nothing easier than to walk about the place as I wished. All I need do, if challenged, was to ask again for the nearest toilet. My real problem was to find some suitable clothes. The rough hospital garments I was wearing would mark me out instantly I tried to quit the place, while my own clothes, even if I could find them, would be little better.

I found myself able to move about with a fair degree of muscular ease, in spite of the bruising I had received from the rocks of the mountain stream. I wondered what had caused me to pass out on the road. Exhaustion and shock, I decided.

It is always difficult to find your way about an unknown large building, and hospitals always seem particularly awkward, as if their architects had been hired to plan a maze. But since it was a military establishment I felt there must somewhere be a plan, mounted like a picture on the wall. I made no attempt at concealment. The thing always in such a situation is to move about as if you own the place. No hesitation at any branching of the corridors, or at any space which has several corridors opening off it. Make an immediate choice of your route, and then move calmly and not too quickly along it. Everybody in a hospital has a job to do. So why should they trouble themselves about you, so long as you don't dither or stagger, or otherwise make a fool of yourself?

I found just such a plan as I was looking for. I studied it just as I've said, as if I owned the establishment, not as if I were lost and anxious to find my way back to my ward. Because I wasn't in the least degree anxious to find my way back, for I had no intention of returning there. My tour about the hospital corridors had already shown me that my balance was not impaired. With the worry of this possible inhibiting factor removed, I saw no reason not to continue as I had planned.

What I was seeking was an area close by an operating theatre. Particularly, I was looking for a dressing room where the theatre staff removed their everyday clothing to put on sterilized surgical wear. My past experience of hospital procedures was helpful to me now. I knew it was a matter of getting the timing exactly right. First, the nurses and the anaesthetists, and then the surgeons. Once they were all occupied it would be easy to find what I was looking for. But should the timing be wrong, should I choose a moment too soon, or too late, then I could hardly escape a challenge in such a sensitive part of the hospital. This sounds more difficult than it was, since all I really had to do was to watch for the WARNING—THEATRE OCCU-PIED red lights, which gave me the right moment without too much of a problem.

Once I found a dressing room I didn't waste too much time about it. Trousers and shoes were the most awkward, because I had to find roughly the right size. I made a quick selection by eye of two possibilities for the trousers. Then I checked them for size, using hand spans, four spans down the inside of the leg. Quickly I pulled on the trousers I had chosen, directly over the top of my bed garments. The jacket by contrast was easy, for I simply took one of the white coats. For effect, I then grabbed a stethoscope, that remarkable symbol of the medical profession, which I wore in the proper style about my neck. For shoes, I did the best I could. They were too tight for doing much walking, but there was no reason why they shouldn't suffice to get me out of the hospital. The trousers were by contrast too full about the middle. Hidden under the jacket this didn't show too much, however.

With this first stage complete, I removed myself quickly from the vicinity of the operating theatre. Strolling now with an almost offensive nonchalance, I was jerked back to reality by the remark of a passing young man of about my own age.

"Been in trouble?" he asked.

"Skiing," I replied.

"Nothing like it" was his cheery response, as he passed me.

The trouble of course was that, while many patients might have bandages around their heads, a bandaged doctor was unusual. By now my absence from my bed would surely have been noticed. Some form of search, perhaps not yet very intense, would have started. But soon it would become a general alert through the hospital. By then I must be rid of the bandage.

I walked past an unattended trolley in one of the corridors, picking up a box of Band-aids as I did so. At the next toilet I removed most of the bandage, leaving the underlying lint over my damaged eye. The now exposed cheek was red and raw, but better than might have been expected, more superficial, I hoped, than the hospital attendants would be looking for. With the help of the Band-aids I fixed the piece of lint in position. I was pleased to find that I was capable of flexing the muscles around the eye again, which suggested that its former jammed condition had been due to severe swelling. Even so, I was still far from being a prepossessing sight. But at least the highly distinctive bandage, suggestive of more extreme injury, was gone. In any case, I had no intention of continuing to pad around the hospital corridors for very much longer.

There were signs marked EXIT, so I simply continued in the directions indicated until I came to a large entrance lobby. I knew I was approaching it from the flower boxes which suddenly appeared in the corridors. There was a desk in the lobby. Without bothering even to glance towards the several clerks, who were occupying themselves with sheaves of papers, I made my way to large swing doors. It had all been very easy.

Outside was a quite large courtyard, with an exit to the wide world beyond through large iron gates. These were flung full open, although they were guarded by a group of helmeted soldiers. I saw no reason why this last step should cause any difficulty. Nor at first did I see any difficulty in the black limousine that swept in through the gate. It came to a stop just before me, a few seconds after I emerged through the swing doors. My trouble was the man who sat beside the driver. He had fair hair, and as he looked towards me I saw that his eyes were cold and of a light-blue color. Thinking that in my new outfit I might have an unexpected look about me, I sought to by-pass the car. I tried to move away, towards the iron gates.

But the man with the English voice had studied me too well, back there in the Moscow University bookstore. In a flash it seemed, the rear door was opened. I stopped beside it, seeing a third man seated there. There was no command or statement from my acquaintance of the light blue eyes.

"Kind of you to offer me a lift," I murmured as I slipped into the vacant rear seat. The door clicked shut and immediately the car swung away, out through the hospital gates.

"It was lucky we didn't keep you waiting," the man beside me said.

"Harvard?" I asked.

"Princeton, actually."

I'd never understood what it was about intelligence agencies that attracted the Ivy League types. But sure enough they always flocked to them, like bees to nectar.

"Where are we going?"

"Ankara."

It was in my mind to ask who had given them the tip-off, but I desisted, if only because the man beside me, an earnest-looking bespectacled individual, might have considered the question too coarsely put.

I was more than a bit mortified by this tip-off, for I'd thought I'd managed my peregrinations through the hospital with a tolerable measure of skill. The best guess I could make was that W.I. must already have had someone there, perhaps several hours before I made my move, perhaps even while I was unconscious. Instead of seeking to question me, which maybe the doctors had vetoed, W.I. had simply waited and watched. I was angry with myself for not guessing that I might be followed back and forth along the hospital corridors and then up to the dressing room beside the operating theatre. I must have been dead easy to follow, because my strategy had been to walk openly, avoiding all temptation to glance behind me. Dead easy. A man with his head in a bandage, and with only one good eye. But at least I was on my way to Ankara, and in good solid comfort at that.

"How's your Russian coming on?" I asked the blue-eyed man.

"It has improved a lot in the last few days" was the reply.

"You'll find it useful," I assured him.

I wondered about taking a swipe at the Princeton man and then putting an arm lock around the neck of my recently Russian-speaking blue-eyed friend. I was tempted to try it, for they must all have thought I was physically much weaker than I really was. Indeed, if I had appreciated just what I was getting into, I think I would almost certainly have had a go, particularly as by this time the driver's attention was fully occupied, since the car was now making good speed through the outskirts of Erzurum.

Yet I had set myself to cause a diversion, and the best possible diversion would be to make W.I. believe that in making my capture they were on to an important development. My wrist watch had been taken away from me in the hospital, along with my clothes, but I had caught a glimpse at a desk calendar in the entrance hall there, just before I came out through the swing doors. From this I knew I had now only a little more than three days to go to complete the week I'd promised Edelstam. I'd little doubt I could bamboozle this fellow beside me for a mere three days. Little I knew.

We had come no great distance before we reached the entrance to a small airstrip. The car moved around various buildings until it stopped beside what seemed like the departure hut. At any rate there were several light planes parked close by, and there were four armed soldiers on duty, as well as two M.P.'s. Not the right place now for me to make a demonstration, I could see.

Without a word I got out of the car, allowing myself to be led to one of the planes. It turned out to be a twin-engined six-seater. Besides me, the M.P.'s escorted the man with light-blue eyes and the Princeton type to it, and then got in themselves. A pilot appeared from out of the building. He paid no attention to any of us, but walked around for a moment checking, it seemed, on the plane, although what there was to check on was unclear. Then he swung himself in an expert way into the cockpit. A moment later first one engine and then the other caught and fired. We waited a few moments, as the revolutions picked up, and then taxied out to the airstrip. A short run, gaining speed, and we were airborne. It was a quick way to Ankara, and a much more comfortable way than I'd expected.

I didn't like the place to which I was taken. I would much have preferred a military jail, with a high-walled perimeter, guarded by dogs, machine guns, and a high-tension electric wire, to the large house in a prosperous quiet avenue. In the beginning it had seemed all very cultured when I was taken through several well-appointed large rooms. But the cell in which I was finally dumped suggested a different situation. It had a small barred window, and its furnishing was merely a plain hard bed. Scarcely good enough for the servant quarters. I was surprised to be taken there, for I had expected to be interrogated immediately. Delay was hardly in my captors' interest.

Gingerly, I removed the strips of adhesive plaster and the lint. The world at first appeared grey as I sought to open my left eye. Then to my delight there was a miraculous moment when the mists dissolved. My trouble with W.I. suddenly appeared minor compared with the fact that I had my sight again. I had survived when I was supposed not to survive. I lay on the bed thinking about that.

It was several hours before they fetched me to the interrogation room. Instantly I guessed the reason for the delay, for seated at a long table, together with my friend from Princeton, was a Russian. You could tell it from his features and his build, from his wooden give-nothing-away expression, and from the many medals which winked and chinked on the left side of his uniform. There were the usual two M.P.'s, armed with carbines, and there were two others whom from their air of self-effacement I correctly guessed to be interpreters.

The Russian began it by asking for an account of my movements since leaving Moscow University. I answered him in Russian, which had to be translated from time to time for the benefit of the Princeton man. I told them how I had taken the train from Moscow to Topolev, Georgia.

"Who was your contact?" the Russian wanted to know. This I knew to be the standard refrain of all interrogations, and I had prepared my answer to it.

"My father," I replied.

When this reply was translated to the Princeton man, he began to rummage about in a large file, flicking the pages as he searched for some document.

"According to our information," he said at length, "your father was killed five years ago, in Idaho, in a mountain accident."

"Nuts. My father was an undercover agent. He spent those five years in Russia."

There was a whispered conversation between the uniformed Russian and one of the interpreters, who then left the room. He returned a few moments later, accompanied by a girl carrying several further files of papers. I must say a word about this girl. She was quite beautiful. I don't mean pretty, or attractive. I mean beautiful, like a vision from classical Greece. It was the sort of beauty you find yourself remembering weeks afterwards, remembering with sadness that the rest of us cannot be like that.

In my limited experience, such girls always have a snag about them. The snag now was that this girl was wearing a Russian army uniform, ranking captain. She handed over the papers, saying, "These are the ones, General." The general nodded with an accompanying chink of his medals, and the girl immediately left us. I was sorry to see her go. I shouldn't have been.

There was a confabulation between my two interrogators, the Princeton man for W.I., and the general for the K.G.B.; Edelstam had said that the West and East had been doing a lot of talking together. In this respect at least he had told me the truth.

"Where is your father now?" the Russian eventually asked.

"Dead."

From the dumb, sullen, disbelieving looks which settled on the faces of my two interrogators, I knew I was easily winning our battle. It was remarkable how effective the truth could be.

"That makes a very convenient story," said the Princeton man. When this was translated to him, the Russian general gave a derisive snort, adding the question, "How was this?"

"My father died in a vast explosion, of which no doubt you are aware. At a place near the Russo-Turkish border. On the Russian side, more or less due east of Lake Cala."

This information wiped the sneers off their faces.

"What was this explosion?" they immediately wanted to know.

"It was caused by the destruction of an Outlander device."

I felt as if I could read the workings of their minds. The sequence was doubt-surprise-consternation-fear. Fear prompted the next question, asked by the Russian general with an attempt at sarcasm, "So the Outlanders entrusted this device to your father, who worked for ten years in Moscow as a trade representative. Or perhaps they entrusted it to you, a mere student. Is that what you are asking us to believe?"

"My father was an Outlander himself," I answered imperturbably. "His real function was to keep a watch on your two governments."

The truth continued to have an unsettling effect on my interrogators. The Princeton man polished his spectacles.

"Why," he asked, "was this explosion arranged so close to the frontier?"

"To enable me to cross immediately into Turkey—in order to report the destruction of the device."

The Russian frowned. "The frontier there is not so easily crossable," he muttered.

"Nor is it," I answered, pointing to my injuries.

My reddened cheek and black, distorted eye must have given me a strangely malevolent look. At any rate I had the clear sensation of grinding my Princeton friend and his Russian colleague as one might grind a powder with mortar and pestle.

"Your father," went on the Russian, "why was he killed?"

"The destruction of the battery-like device was of necessity a calculated risk."

"No man likes to die."

"My father was not a man. He was an Outlander. He did his duty," I replied with a coldness that I felt. "His sacrifice will not be forgotten, when the reckoning comes to be made," I added, rising from the chair they'd given me and standing glaring down at them.

"I suppose you understand that we shall test your story?" the Princeton man said.

"By which I suppose you mean that you will report to your governments the full seriousness of their predicament. You are both now in a fair way to having your power supply cut off."

When this had been translated to the Russian by one of the interpreters, he whispered back to the interpreter, who whispered in turn to the American. The American nodded to the Russian. Then he turned to me.

"You will be held for further enquiries," he said in a toneless voice. With a further nod, the two men rose from the long desk and quitted the room, accompanied by the two interpreters, leaving me guarded by the two M.P.'s. But not for long. An orderly appeared holding a sheet of paper, which he showed to the M.P.'s. A few moments later I found myself back again in my cell, with its small barred window and with its solitary bed for furnishing.

I lay on the bed again, congratulating myself on having set the cat among the pigeons in a most satisfactory style. Reports would be made to the political authorities, who would now be forced, as I saw it, to order my release. From here on, as I saw it, it would be the red-carpet treatment all the way. My attention turned itself to the Russian girl, and to what might be the best way of securing her acquaintance.

What I did not see, as I lay there, was how little my own fate weighed in the balance. Even my total disappearance would hardly make a bad case much worse for the political governments of West and East. It must therefore have seemed logical to put my story to the ultimate test, just in case the battery device might not have been destroyed, which in fact it hadn't been. From this point of view, indeed from every point of view, I was expendable. There must have been a blockage in my mind which prevented me from anticipating the ordeal that now lay before me.

The first hint that I was to be forced to play to a different script came when I was taken in a small lift down into the basement of the house. There I found the man with the light-blue eyes. I always thought of him as an Englishman, but that was from the way he spoke. He had the sort of accent which started the war of '76.

To my surprise I also found the Russian girl, which made me think for a moment that this basement place wasn't what I'd supposed it to be. I resolved to put the matter to the test,

"Hi, Sadie," I said, grinning. "Remember the time we danced together? At Olaf's place?"

So saying I gave her backside a tweak.

The girl wheeled on me with remarkable speed, delivering a whack across my face as she did so. It was also remarkable in its strength for such a light person, especially as it came unerringly on the injured part of my face.

Which showed I'd been right all along. This basement of a pleasant-looking house, in a pleasant-looking street, was just exactly where I'd no wish to be.

"O.K., Sadie," I muttered through the pain, "that's one for the book."

I decided I didn't like the girl after all. I didn't like the hefty muscular types who always seemed to be hanging around me. I didn't like the blue-eyed Englishman, even when he said, "Play chess?"

There was a board with men set up on a small table, which he indicated with a gesture.

"Sure," I answered, taking a seat at the table.

I'd played chess once or twice before, in a crude beginner's bungling way. In sitting there, offering myself up for the slaughter, as I thought, it wasn't chess I wanted to play. It was time I was playing for now. About two more days, forty-eight hours I reckoned, would take me to the end of Edelstam's week. From here on, every minute, every hour, I knew would be important. So I had no hesitation at all in passing a little of those forty-eight hours in bungling my way through a game of chess.

My mistake had been in hauling myself out of that mountain stream. My father had known when his time had come, and he had gone with good grace. So should I have gone. It would have taken but a few seconds, bouncing down the rocks and over the waterfall. Then these intelligence people would have had no conceivable lead to go on. Instead they now had me, for forty-eight hours. Oddly enough, in spite of this analysis, in spite of my conviction that the incident of the waterfall had been known to Edelstam, I still believed that some help would eventually come my way, after a week. This had been the agreement, which I had a strange inner conviction would be honored.

It was also strange that I didn't play chess at all in a puerile, bungling way. It was as if some new range of perception had suddenly been switched on within me, something which I had never needed before, but which I needed now. I do not know at what level of perception I actually played, for I have no knowledge of the Englishman's ability. All I know is that his schemes seemed trivially clear to me, and that from the first move onward I had the conviction that his defeat was inevitable.

It was while I was contemplating the final *coup de grâce* that the Englishman struck me. The blow was delivered with the speed of a skilled boxer. I had just sufficient warning of its coming to flick my head, so that the point of impact came on the right side, avoiding the already injured area. I sprawled away from the table, the game instantly forgotten.

I had the good sense to lie there prostrate on the floor. Strong hands half carried, half dragged me—ten, twenty, maybe thirty paces. Then I was wedged into a contained area. A heavy door thundered close by and the light went out. Realising that I was alone, I tried to stand, but the box I was in came no higher than my shoulders. My bent position being uncomfortable, I sat down. I endured the cold for perhaps five minutes and then got hastily to my feet, hitting my head on the roof. I was in an icebox, a 'cooler.' I lay on my right side and tried to will the circulation back into my numbed feet.

The routine seemed to be to keep on the move, never letting any part of the body become too chilled. I worked out a rota system, trying to keep each part of me from being in contact with the cold floor for too long. Time stood still. Forty-eight hours was an eternity, an impossible dream. Forty-eight minutes had become a scarcely attainable target.

Even in my befuddled state, I saw that it was not my captors' intention for me to survive. The consequences of releasing me now would be exceedingly drastic. They would keep me alive only so long as it was believed I might be a source of important information. Hence it followed that I must neither reveal everything I knew, nor must I let my captors become convinced that I knew nothing. Only by giving them an objective, by permitting them to work on me, could I remain alive. It was at this point that I lost consciousness.

Intense bright lights suddenly pierced the darkness. The air I was breathing felt stiflingly hot.

"Who are you?" an unknown voice boomed, seemingly within my ears and head.

"Peter," I heard myself reply in a faint, faraway sound.

"Who is your contact?" The voice came again, like thunder all around my head.

"The easiest turn in skiing is . . ." I heard myself whisper.

"What is your connexion with the Outlanders?"

"Skiing is beautiful," came my distant murmur. I willed myself to think about skiing. Anything about skiing. I kept on faintly saying, "Skiing, skiing, skiing . . ." forcing myself to allow no other thought to enter my brain.

The questions stopped as abruptly as they had begun. The lights went out, and silence enveloped me once more.

Then it started again, for I became aware of the coldness of the floor of the small box once more. But now I was no longer sure what position I was in, whether sitting, crouching on one side or the other, or stooping with the back of my neck arched against the roof of the box. I knew that at the next interrogation I must give just a little, just sufficient to keep them hoping for more. I searched my mind for some topic of relevance, but a topic already known to my captors. A vision of Professor Ortov swam into my disordered consciousness. From this, I willed myself to babble about the art forms of Byzantium, which was where it had all started.

The second interrogation was similar to the first. I tried shouting my replies, but still my voice sounded faint and distant in my head, an effect of the drugs they were using on me. The unknown voice of the questioner roared through my whole being, insistently demanding the one simple thing, the identity of my contact. Afterwards I realised it would have been impossible for anybody in my condition to have delivered complex information. Since I certainly did not have the battery device my captors were seeking, their hope of finding it could lie only with my contact.

Another thing I realised afterwards was that I suffered no psychological deterioration. The sense of revolt was strong in me. I desperately wanted out of my fuddled state, out of the pain and out of the cold. But my interrogators did not succeed in imposing their nightmare world on my inner consciousness, as I think they would have done with a human. I was still sharply aware of the battery thing, of the need to protect Edelstam. I gave my captors information about Byzantine art forms, highly cultured no doubt, but not what they were seeking. But then the voice boomed once more through my consciousness, telling me that the box to which I was returning was cold . . . cold . . . cold. Endlessly cold.

So it was. On my third immersion in the box, I was not only unaware of my position, but my hands could no longer detect any sensation in my legs. I was desperately afraid that the cooling was carrying me close to death. There was nothing in my mind now, except that I was expendable. I could form no plan for the third interrogation. I was expendable, and the sooner I died the better for me. In death would be my ultimate revolt, my victory.

Suddenly a searing pain spread everywhere through my body, convincing me that here at last were the final pangs. Then my fingers reached out and touched my skin. Miraculously, there was feeling in the fingers again. I moved my arm. There was a dragging resistance to it, from which it at last dawned on me that I was immersed in hot water. Two vague grey splotches were looking down on me, which I took to be faces. I was aware of needles pricking into my arm. Then I felt myself lifted from the water. For a moment I had the sensation of being rubbed down, before the world exploded into light and colour.

Not that this worried me. I felt I understood exactly what was happening, and in the understanding of it I knew myself to be devilishly clever. I wanted to laugh at my own exceeding cleverness, a phenomenon of nature. Not remotely did I know now where I was, or who the people about me were. Only my cleverness was important. I knew I had tricked them all. Yes, that was it, the key to everything. I had tricked them all. The whole world would laugh with me when they knew about it. Everybody would laugh. To laugh. That was the only important thing in the whole wide world. Endlessly to laugh, to laugh, and still to laugh.

Slowly my brain returned to more coherent operation. Bit by bit the normal inhibitory gates re-established themselves, and bit by bit I knew who I was, and where I was, and who the people about me were. And with this returning rationality I began to feel cold once more. I seemed unable to move, up or down or sideways. There seemed to be no way I could gain relief from the burning cold. There were no interrogators now, so why didn't they just kill me right away, why this endless searing pain?

Very slowly, one small degree by degree, the pain moderated, to be replaced by the first flush of warmth. Deliciously, I luxuriated in the spreading warmth. It was as if the cold had made my nerves more sensitive than usual. Over my body there was a light caressing. I became aware that I was not alone. In a dim light I could see the beautiful features of the girl who had swiped me so viciously on the face. She was swiping me no longer. Her hands were moving everywhere. I tried to reach out and grab hold of her, but my motor system was drugged into inactivity. So there was nothing to stop her from exercising her will on me. As the sensations of warmth and excitement became more and more intense, the girl's voice sounded in my ears. It was caressing in tone, like her hands, but it was far louder than a natural voice. It seemed to come commandingly from afar off.

The question was insistently the same, a demand for the name of my contact.

"Dolfuss," I moaned at last, "Dolfuss!"

This was only the beginning. The demands went on and on, always the demands for more information. Weakly, I thought now only to prolong the delicious warmth. I responded more and more to the commanding voice, coming to me from its distant Olympian height.

As my knowledge of the affair came out in mumbling phrases, as tortuously as I could make it, I was at first suffused by shame at my own weakness in giving them anything at all. Then, as I detected increasing frustration in the questioning voice, I realised that, accurate as much of my information might be, it was singularly useless to my captors. All I had to do in my story was to replace Edelstam by the mysterious Dolfuss. Dolfuss was thus my contact from the moment I crossed the pass. For a description of Dolfuss I gave that of the man from the Pushkin Museum. Of Dolfuss's present whereabouts I could offer no answer, for in truth I knew no answer. It was a story well calculated to puzzle, even though it contained a deal that was correct. I managed to wonder how much of the forty-eight hours had passed.

At length, other voices came to me loudly, but seemingly from afar off. I heard the girl say, "There's nothing more left in him."

"Are you absolutely sure?" It was the Englishman speaking.

"Absolutely. He has taken much more than would be normal. The experience was very strong."

A new voice cut in. "If you're both fully satisfied, I'll despatch him then."

"You have your orders, Doctor?" the girl asked.

"Yes, for despatch and immediate cremation."

There was a rustle of papers, sounding in my ears like a gale in a forest.

"Poor bastard. He played chess quite well," the Englishman said.

"But not well enough," the doctor replied with a laugh.

I heard the receding sound of shoes. There was something about the pace of it which told me it was the girl.

"Goodbye, Sadie," I managed to croak, before there was a prick of a needle in my arm.

"That should do it," the doctor remarked in an unconcerned tone.

"Poor bastard," the Englishman repeated.

I was surprised that I didn't lose consciousness. Instead, I felt an inner numbing spread everywhere through my body, as if I had taken a heavy dose of some swift-acting hemlock. Hands untied a number of nylon strips with which I had been bound. A head looked down at me while fingers prodded my eyeballs. I tried to move but nothing functioned.

"O.K.?" was the Englishman's last question, in his normal voice.

"O.K." was the reply, again in a normal voice, from which I deduced that electronic equipment had been removed from my head.

I was lifted on to a trolley. In a strange way, although I was completely paralysed, I could hear and see with clarity, my eyelids having been left open. Then I was covered by a sheet, and the trolley began to move, taking me on my last journey, to the crematorium. I tried desperately to cry out to the men who had been detailed so to transport me, but no sound came from my lips, even though thoughts filled my brain with an intense and fast-pulsing horror.

We soon stopped, at a lift which took us upwards, to a floor that opened from the lift with a clattering of metal gates. The sheet was whisked away and I was immediately lifted into a wooden coffin.

"Going stiff already," muttered one of the attendants.

The removal of the cloth had given me a momentary range of vision, in which I could see from the tail of my eye a second body lying on a white plastic-covered table. Then my vision was cut away by the wooden sides of the coffin. A lid was quickly slotted into position, fastened it seemed by four wing nuts.

I tried again to shout, and then to knock with my hand on the coffin lid, but without the smallest effect. A voice said, "This is the one for dissection."

"No, he's for cremation" was the reply.

Something pressed on the coffin lid, and there was a thump.

"We'll take it from here," the first voice continued in a rumbling bass tone.

"O.K."

"O.K."

I wondered what could be so right about it all. There was more thumping.

"Lot of business today," came another voice.

"Seems like they've been having a busy time," the bass one replied.

Without warning my coffin was suddenly lifted.

"Now then, be careful there. Can't have him bumped about."

At this witticism there was a burst of laughter, from which I deduced there must be at least three of them in this morgue-like place. I was then carried along in fits and starts, interrupted by the opening and closing of doors. Down a flight of stairs, and then more carrying. I wondered how it was possible to conceal a crematorium in a respectable-looking house in such a respectable-looking street.

Heavy doors thudded, and an engine sprang to life. This was the answer—the crematorium was situated somewhere different.

"Papers," I heard a new voice say. There was the sound of heavy boots on gravel. The doors were opened and someone put a hand on the coffin. Then the same sequence in reverse, doors closed, boots on gravel.

"Everything in order?" was the question, in the rumbling bass voice from the morgue.

"Just checking. Can't be too careful."

"I guess not."

"O.K. Be on your way."

The engine revved, and with a further cry back and forth, we were on our way. After we had gone perhaps a mile, the vehicle stopped, the doors opened, and my coffin was manhandled outside. I knew we were outside because a brighter light came through a small chink at a point where the lid did not fit quite snugly with the sides of the coffin. The attendants gave a heave-ho and I was swung on to some kind of platform. This was followed by a further clang of steel on steel. Convinced that I was now on a form of conveyor belt which would glide its way to the fires of the crematorium, I waited in a choked, pounding terror.

My body started to move, causing the thudding in my head to become more violent still. But then there came a quick acceleration, followed by a changing of gear, of the further vehicle in which I now realised I had been placed. All these moves seemed too mysterious to work out, so I did the only thing possible. I waited. I waited for the second vehicle to stop again. Perhaps the crematorium was situated on the outskirts of Ankara. It might even be a public crematorium. Perhaps I was to be destroyed in full public view, unable to make my plight known to anyone there.

The journey went on, farther than I expected. I found

the delay irritating. Better to get it over, I kept telling myself. Every added moment only increased the anguish.

Someone climbed into the rear of the vehicle. Light suddenly flooded into the coffin as the lid was removed. A face was thrust close by my own. In a moment it withdrew, leaving the lid open.

"He looks done for. He's been given too much," I heard a voice say.

"Better give him a shot then" was the reply in the bass voice I'd learned to recognize. The face reappeared a moment later.

"All right then, slow down for a minute," I heard it mutter. The vehicle braked down to a crawl. In the corner of my eye I saw the glint of a needle, but I felt no sensation of its being stuck into me. The face withdrew for a second time, and immediately we were on the move again.

The journey lasted for perhaps two hours. We bumped for a while over a rough track. I could see trees close by. Soon thereafter we stopped. A moment later the two men lifted the coffin out of what I could now see to be an ambulance. Then, putting on the lid, they carried me some way through the trees, to a small shack. There to my relief the lid was removed once more.

"Doesn't look to be any reaction," said the man who'd given me the injection.

"We can't hang about. We've got little time" was the bass response.

"I don't like to see his eyes open like that."

"Easily dealt with," said the driver, bending down and closing my eyelids. I tried again to shout to him to leave my eyes open, but no sound came. All I could see now was the faint glimmer which penetrated through the eyelids themselves. The door of the shack was banged shut. There was a momentary sound of footsteps, followed by the closing of the ambulance doors. The engine started up, revved for a moment, and then died away as the ambulance returned along the track back to the highway. In my paralysed state, I had no sense of touch, no smell, no sight. My only awareness of the world was of the wind faintly stirring the trees outside the shack.

Night came. This I knew because even the faint glow of light through my eyelids disappeared. I had no contact with the world now, except for the occasional creaking of the timber of the shack and for slight sounds which came to me from the forest outside. Without these, I would soon have relapsed into unconsciousness. I struggled to give attention to these sounds, but it was hard to stop my thoughts from wandering off on their own.

Who and what were the Outlanders? Where had they come from? Where was their 'home'? According to my father, I was an Outlander myself. But this knowledge only served to heighten the sense of mystery. I decided that if I were ever to come safely out of my present predicament I would do what I could toward answering these questions, whatever the cost might be. What had happened to my father at the moment of the explosion? Had he, like me, escaped death in some remarkable way?

While pondering these further questions, I must have in fact become unconscious for a while, indeed for many hours. I awoke, immediately aware of a difference. It took some seconds there in the darkness of night to realise what it was. My eyelids had blinked. Slowly as time passed I experienced the return of sensation in my finger tips, first in one finger then in another. The sensation progressed from the faintest impression to a fierce tingling which made my hands feel as if they were on fire. Then half hour by half hour my limbs began to move once more. I tried to sit up in the coffin but found I had not the strength to do so. I made noises with my mouth but I still could not control the muscles of my lips, so there was no coherent speech, only gasps, grunts, and whining noises. I managed to raise an arm and to touch my lips with the fingers. They had the same numbness about them that you get after the injection of a local anaesthetic.

The light of dawn had not long been faintly suffusing the interior of the hut when I heard a sound which grew rapidly from a distant murmur to an ominous roar. My instinct for self-preservation sought to force my arms and legs to action. I half raised my body within the coffin, and at that precise moment the shed door opened with a crash. There in front of me was a huge man dressed in dungarees with a trench coat. He had a kind of bulldog face with deep brown eyes, which now stared down upon me.

"What the hell am I to do with a corpse that isn't a corpse?" he rumbled to himself.

I tried to reply, but could only manage to get out a horrible wailing sound. At this the fellow stooped down and simply picked me up in his arms as if I were a small child.

The early-morning sky outside glinted through dense foliage. The big man carried me for a way along the track, to where a battered old truck stood mutely in a pool of light mist. I was thumped down on the ground while the rear end of the vehicle was opened up. I was then hoisted through the open tailgate. The big fellow jumped up himself, to drag me the length of the flooring, until my back was placed firmly against the driver's cab. Next he threw

90

quantities of evil-smelling straw on top of me. A moment later the tailgate was closed with a clang, and my curious companion began to sing to himself as he hauled himself into the driver's seat. With a monstrous clatter the ancient vehicle came to life, and in a moment we were bumping our way, more boisterously than I would have preferred, out of the forest on to a highway—at least I deduced from the smoother ride of it that a highway had been reached.

The morning light strengthened as the truck roared on and on, up and down the grades of the road. And all the time the rigidity within me was softening. My arms and legs were beginning to flex themselves with a show of muscle, and my lips could now detect the pressure of my fingers.

I was trying to sit up when we came to a shuddering halt, which threw me back deep among the straw.

"Papers?" I heard a voice ask.

"You people never think about anything but papers" was my driver's grumbling response. There was a crisp sound as a document of some kind was produced.

"Pigs to Ankara," came the first voice.

I heard men moving on the roadway. From beneath the straw I sensed them looking in.

"Quite a stink you've got in there," a new voice remarked.

"Load of pigs" was my driver's placid response.

"Rather you than me," said the first voice, with a laugh.

There was another mighty roar and clatter and our ancient vehicle lurched into motion once more. After a further hour or so, during which time I was content to remain covered by the straw, the barely tolerable ride of the truck changed into a rolling and pitching motion. Shortly thereafter, we came again to a halt. The door of the cab opened. Clumsily I was getting to my feet as my great hulk of a driver opened the rear,

"Not often a corpse comes to life again," he rumbled.

With the fellow's help I managed to slither to the ground outside.

"Try to put these on while I attend to this machine," he said, handing me a peasant's rough overcoat and a wool hat. First, I put on the hat, then slowly the coat. My companion was pouring gasoline into the old tub of a truck from cans which appeared to have been stored there, the place being another clearing in a piece of woodland. While he completed the job, I walked back and forth, moving jerkily like a puppet.

"It will be all right to have you up front from here on," the big man said. He helped me up into the cab, for I was still unable to do anything more than shuffle.

For several hours thereafter we drove over twisting hilly roads, stopping once more for gasoline, which had evidently also been cached at another prearranged point on our route. All the time the big man played a radio at full volume, which not only frayed my nerves but served to prevent me from asking the many questions which occupied my mind.

Gradually the hills became less dry. Running water appeared in the stream beds, and there were new green grass and early spring flowers in the meadows which opened up before us from time to time. It was at one such meadow that we turned at last along a farm lane, which led after a kilometre or two to a group of buildings.

The big fellow swung the truck in front of a low-built farmhouse. No sooner had he tumbled out of the cab than a girl erupted from the house. In a few strides she reached the big man and clutched him with wide-open arms. Meanwhile I eased myself from the cab, careful that my legs should not collapse beneath me. Feeling like a clockwork doll, I stepped awkwardly to where the girl was still hugging the big man. I did so, not so much to break up the clinch, but because there was something oddly familiar about this girl. Indeed, as soon as she looked towards me, she gave a smile. A moment later she was kissing my cheeks, holding me with a vigour that almost threw me off my unsteady legs. As she then moved a foot or two away from me, I saw the dimples appear in her cheeks. It was the clerk from the Moscow University bookstore.

"And who might you be?" I asked the big man.

There was a rumble of laughter.

"I go by many names," he said, "but for you—you may call me Dolfuss."

"My only real problem was to determine your serum type," Dolfuss explained to me some hours later, after I had managed to eat some dinner without ill effects.

"I had to be sure the death injection they use would induce a catatonic state in you," he continued. "It is a delicate difference of chemistry between a human and an Outlander."

I found it odd to listen to the big man speaking in this way. My first impression of Dolfuss, as a hulking farmer with his ancient truck and his load of pigs, was hard to slough away.

"But it is my speciality, so you had no cause to worry."

This seemed to me too light-hearted a view of my former situation, but I refrained from saying so.

"You see," Dolfuss rumbled, "it is very hard to extract

anybody who is alive. But every agency becomes careless once it is believed that a person is dead. It is my speciality," he repeated.

"Will they be looking for me now?"

"No, no, no! How should that be? It is believed that you are cremated. Would they be looking for smoke then?"

"But I wasn't cremated."

"Ah, now! But some person was! A person whom it was planned to dissect. It will be for him that they will now be looking. Eh? Perhaps you don't understand?"

I remembered the other body in the morgue-like place.

"So you switched the bodies?"

"Only the labels on the coffins. It was not necessary to be dramatic."

"Where is Edelstam?" I asked, abruptly changing the subject.

For answer, Dolfuss put the first finger of his right hand to his lips. "Shush," he said, "we do not mention the gentleman. But in confidence I will tell you that his mission has been accomplished."

"So I can consider myself free then?"

"If it pleases you to follow the same route I will make arrangements for it. That's why you were brought to this place."

"Follow Edelstam! I certainly have a few points to take up with him."

"Doubtless. It is a way that he has," Dolfuss observed drily.

"I don't see how I can return to the U.S.A., or to Russia."

"You would need to change your function to a clandestine role." This remark of Dolfuss's made me wonder just what I'd been doing over the past few months. When I

plied to me for that matter. I'd been a specialist who'd done exactly what I was asked to do. Were the others among us also specialists? Was my father a specialist? Was it his speciality to work the battery device? For the life of me I'd not been able to see how to work the damn thing. There had been no obvious visible controls to it, just the continuing iridescence about it. So how the devil could it be worked? Yet my father had done so without difficulty. On the other hand, my father had not been able to cross the pass, because crossing the pass was not his speciality. It was mine. And what was Edelstam's speciality which had made it necessary for him then to relieve me of the thing?

I racked my brains without success on this last question, and in doing so I came to a much bigger problem. If we were all thus fitting ourselves into some pattern, how had the pattern itself come to be laid down? By the Outlanders presumably. And yet we were all Outlanders. So was there an Outlander somewhere whose speciality it was to plan, to make patterns? If so, I had a fancy it would be interesting to seek out this planner, this mover-around of lesser specialists like myself. Just as I had been given to barging around wild country in a fairly carefree manner, I thought I might try barging around on a bigger scale. Outside the Earth, assuming this super-figure to be located outside, in the 'home' of the Outlanders—which seemed a reasonable presumption. Putting it crudely, I decided I would do my damnedest to find out what it was that made this super-figure tick. Who was it who really understood the battery thing? Who had made it in the first place? Who controlled the power beams to the Earth? These were the questions I must try to answer. The attempt would take me into an entirely new phase of my life.

When I eventually told Dolfuss that I'd decided to continue in my own instinctive style, and that I must now make my way 'home,' he nodded gravely.

"It is the wisest decision for you, Peter. You would not have been happy in my kind of life. You see I am happy myself to arrange the details for your journey as far as the space station. But you would not be happy arranging such details. It is not your style, I think."

"If you mean playing tricks on the intelligence agencies, I suppose it isn't," I admitted. Indeed, after my recent experiences, I'd no wish ever to meet up with any intelligence agency, Princeton types or otherwise.

"The shoemaker should stick to his last." Dolfuss nodded sagely. "Besides," he went on, tapping his head, "I have a strong presentiment that you still have very important work to do."

"Did you know my father?" I asked.

A broad smile spread across the big rugged face. "Ah! Your father was a man for the things which interest me. But it is not a case of like father like son, I think. If it was so, the world would be only a dull place."

I could draw him out no further on the subject. The first principle of intelligence work was evidently to say nothing but the things which needed to be said. What was irrelevant to the immediate issue might turn out to be dangerous. This seemed to be the philosophy, which was one of the reasons why I was unhappy with it. I liked to learn and to know, in an easy-going sort of way, which you never could do in this tight-lipped kind of business.

Changing the subject, I asked abruptly, "How do you propose to get me out?"

The question was evidently more to Dolfuss's taste, but even so he was maddeningly indefinite in his answer.

"It depends," he replied.

"On what?"

"On that eye of yours."

"It's going to be all right."

"Oh-ho, yes. It will be all right. No doubt. But the question is whether it will be all right soon enough."

"For what?"

"So that we don't miss the boat."

As if this were a profound witticism, Dolfuss gave a long rumbling laugh. Perceiving that I could get no more from him, I gave the matter up. He would tell me precisely what I needed to know, and not a word more. It was the nature of the specialist.

The healing of my cheek was coming along well, as I'd expected it would, but the whole region around the eye was still blackened, giving me a stage-pirate kind of look. The shaping of the eye socket itself had been slightly changed, so that from here on my whole face would have a somewhat unsymmetrical appearance about it, the kind of peculiarity which a cartoonist seizes upon. The good thing was that the bad headaches which I'd suffered at first had by now disappeared. Sure, I was going to be all right, but would I be all right soon enough to suit Dolfuss and his plans, whatever they might be? I was damned if I knew.

From here on Lena plied me almost constantly with various salves and poultices. I was sceptical of their value, but at least they did no harm, and they gave me the opportunity to find out a bit about Lena herself. She knew nothing of Edelstam, so evidently her photograph, the one shown to me so long ago, had been used without her knowledge. I'd been surprised, from my first day at the farm, that she and Dolfuss conversed together in Turkish, which had had the effect of isolating me, presumably intentionally so. Now I discovered that Lena had a surprising facility in many languages. Beyond her simple statement that languages had been her main interest and study throughout her education in Moscow, I could discover nothing more. Yet plainly her abilities were quite above normal, as if she too were in her own way a specialist. I also found her to be almost entirely without nervous apprehension. The incident in the bookstore, her hoodwinking of the man with ice-blue eyes, had caused her no concern at all. With these qualities, I could see she would be a splendid acquisition for Dolfuss and his organization. It would be hard for anyone to resist her warm, innocent-looking, friendly smile. For me, she had a sort of sisterly affection, but to my loss nothing more.

The day came when Dolfuss examined my eye. He sat me down on a chair, and then padded around the room, gazing at me from various angles. Then he moved the chair to change the lighting, and did the same thing again. Big as he was, he contrived to move with an almost catlike silence, in astonishing contrast to the heavy-footed Edelstam. At last he stood in front of me, nodding repeatedly.

"Perhaps it will be good enough," he said.

I wanted to ask for what, but knowing such a question would surely go unanswered, I asked instead, "There is still time enough?"

Dolfuss went on nodding, a slight frown on his bulldog face. "Yes," he replied, "I think there is still time."

"Time is of the essence," I added, for the sake of something.

"To be at the right place at the right time, that is all important. To be at the wrong place at the wrong time, that is disaster. Like putting yourself in the path of an oncoming truck," Dolfuss continued in a grave fashion.

"When do we move?"

"Tomorrow, I think it will be. Tomorrow already."

I spent my last afternoon at the farm walking the fields which stretched upwards for about a kilometre from the buildings until they reached the lower edge of an extensive belt of woodland. A small brook splashed its way out of the wood and down the sunlit grass, its banks rich in spring flowers. I sat for a long hour beside it, thinking once more of what might lie ahead.

I had a strong presentiment that a kind of death was upon me. Not the sort of complete death which had been planned for me in the respectable house in the respectable avenue back in Ankara. Nor the sort of spectacular death I would have suffered if the avalanche I'd started on my descent from the frontier pass had taken me over the precipice below. A lesser death than these perhaps, but a death in which I would never see the flowers of spring again, or water flowing brightly across a sunlit meadow. As I lay on the warm grass I knew now the full meaning of bitter-sweet. I had an urge to stay on there, hour after hour, savoring indefinitely this last moment, and I had a counter-urge to be up and away, and so to put an end to the torment of it.

The following morning Dolfuss had me dress up in a set of overalls. Lena gave me a smiling kiss on each cheek.

Then we were away, in the same old battered truck as before, climbing up and down on a hill track which took us repeatedly in and out of the woodland. I tried to decide whether it was the same track as the one by which we had come, but I could reach no firm conclusion, because after a while all such tracks come to have the same look about them.

I sat beside Dolfuss in the cab, since we really did have a load of pigs on this occasion. All the time I could both smell them and hear them as they squealed incessantly behind me. I wondered if Dolfuss always used the same battered truck and the same pig gag. Then, once again in a patch of woodland, he brought the truck to a grinding halt.

"Time to be changing," he said, as he heaved himself out of the cab.

I followed along a faint side track through the trees until we reached an elevated metallic structure which looked like a small water tower. Parked beside it was a green tradesman's van. Without hesitation Dolfuss crammed his great bulk into the driver's seat, hunching himself over the wheel. I took the seat beside him, wondering what was going to happen to the pigs.

Sooner or later, I expected my companion to impart a few instructions to me. Instead of doing so, he once again switched on a radio at full volume. Since he paid much attention to it, I decided that maybe he was listening for some message, and not merely seeking to suppress any questions I might otherwise have asked. If there was any such message, it was not apparent, for no sign of animation flickered across my companion's craggy face. He simply drove on and on, hunched up and listening.

We emerged eventually from the country lanes on to a

paved road. There were several junctions, at each of which we always took the larger alternative. Eventually from the road signs I deduced that we were on our way back to Ankara, which seemed to me to be neither safe nor sensible.

Gradually the traffic built up, until it became a steady stream as we reached the outskirts of the city. Suddenly reaching out a huge paw of a hand, Dolfuss flicked off the radio. Now, I thought, the man is going to tell me something. Instead, Dolfuss started to sing. The words, being in Turkish, still told me nothing.

We made our way into what was clearly the prosperous residential section of Ankara, coming at last to a large house with well-kept gardens, naturally in a respectable avenue. Dolfuss swung the van through open gates, up a short gravel drive, bringing us to a halt at the rear of the house.

"Out" was his curt command.

He opened up the back of the van. There on the floor was a workman's bag of tools.

"Pick 'em up, and then go to the tradesman's entrance" were all the instructions I ever received. As my workman's boots crunched over the gravel, I heard the doors of the van slam behind me. The motor was still running. In seconds, the van pulled away and was gone. As I walked the last few paces to what seemed to be the only rear entrance to the house, and which therefore must be the tradesman's entrance, I realised that come what might it would be impossible for me to retrace the way back to the farm in the hills. I was on my own again. Dolfuss had completed his job.

I knocked with a firm fist on the rear door. Quick steps sounded on the other side. Then the door was flung open to reveal a woman of perhaps fifty, of ample girth, who immediately launched herself into a stream of Turkish. Understanding only the scolding tone she was using, I grinned sheepishly down at her. Still not pausing for a word she led me into the house, where I stood holding my bag of tools, while she went off, calling out loudly as she did so.

A moment later she was back with a freckle-faced girl of about seventeen, dressed as a maid. The girl nodded as she received some instruction, while I nodded with her in sympathy. Then she led me through what I could see were the kitchen quarters, with the older woman continuing to call out afterwards in what I took to be a derisive voice.

We came out into a marble-floored large hall. All around me were sundry archaeological finds, old pots and simple metal work for the most part, but in a special cabinet we passed some interesting fine jewellery in silver and gold. My boots cracked on the marble floor and on the steps of a curving flight which took us to the upper levels of the house. No matter how much I sought to tread delicately I failed to suppress the steady thump-thump-thump of my boots, to a degree where I could only compare my ineptitude with that of the ponderous-footed Edelstam.

The freckle-faced girl had a half-frightened look about her. Without speaking, as if to speak would have been above her station, she led me into a corridor, thankfully laid with a deep carpet. We progressed now silently along there for a while. Then the girl knocked on a door. After listening for a response, and there being none, she tentatively opened the way into a luxuriously appointed room on the front side of the house, looking out through big windows on the gardens outside. Upon a large bed a suit of dark clothes had been laid out, as if by a valet. A smaller dressing room and bathroom could be seen adjoining.

The girl said something, which again I didn't understand. Then she pointed, and I saw a damp patch on the carpet immediately below the cock of an old-fashioned water-filled radiator. The girl touched her finger to the bottom of the radiator and it came away with several water drops on it. I grinned and rattled the tool bag ostentatiously, at which the girl said something further and then withdrew, leaving me to fix the radiator.

The trouble was obviously a washer which wasn't seating quite properly. It took but a moment to tighten a nut at the base of the cock, at the point where it entered the main water pipe. Then I wiped the bottom of the radiator dry, and waited to see if any more water accumulated there. It didn't.

I walked quickly back and forth through the adjoining rooms, thinking it ridiculous to call in a workman to fix such a small job. I tested the bathroom fittings. They all seemed perfectly in order. An odd thought occurred to me, so I continued to run the bath water. I stripped off, shaved with a razor I found there, and then slipped into the bath. After lying there for a while, I had just climbed out and was beginning to towel myself dry when I heard noises in the main room. Thinking to find myself in a position of some embarrassment, I waited. The noises continued for perhaps a minute and then stopped. I waited for a further minute before making my way, draped in the towel, to the main room. A shirt, underwear, and a tie had been added to the suit on the bed, and remarkably enough my bag of tools had disappeared.

Remarkably too, the clothes laid out there fitted me well. I dressed without haste, since this was the first time within more than six months that I'd put on anything except crude garments. Merely dressing so was an experience in itself, by now an essentially forgotten luxury. I had just about finished when there came a discreet tap on the outer door.

"Come in," I said in a raised voice—there seemed nothing else I could do. The door opened. Standing there was a man in evening dress, looking for all the world like an old-fashioned butler.

"Mr. Blackwood will see you as soon as you're ready, sir," he said, and was then gone before I could reply, the door closing with a faint, discreet click.

Wondering who the hell Mr. Blackwood might be, I finished adjusting my tie. Looking at myself in a mirror, I began to see the point of Dolfuss's worry over my appearance. Too ghastly a countenance would not have seemed right in the refined, butler-strewn society of Mr. Blackwood. While I still had a distinctly bashed quality, it contrived to give me a tolerable cavalry-officer-about-club look, which I thought would probably pass muster in the upper stratum into which I seemed to have been so curiously precipitated.

I quitted the room, taking care to remember which one it was. The butler was no great distance from my door, as if he had been waiting there for me to emerge. He started off as soon as I appeared, so I simply followed him, about eight paces behind. The upper floors of the house all seemed to be well carpeted, so we made no sound, except when we descended the flight of marble steps. All around

105

me was further evidence of the archaeological activities of my unexpected host. Down the steps we made our way along another carpeted passageway, until we reached a wide doorway which opened into a large room lined on three walls by bookshelves. An open wood fire was burning, and seated beside it was a dignified white-haired man of maybe fifty-five. He was slenderly built, standing an inch or so taller than I was. He came to meet me with an outstretched hand.

"Ah, Peter!" he exclaimed. "Glad to see you. Ralph Blackwood. I've just bought a few Byzantine icons I'd like your opinion on."

So I'd become an art critic now. Inclining my head, I said I'd be glad to take a look at his icons. The subject of icons is no simple one, as may be judged from the fact that Blackwood's mention of them had immediately explained all the curious events which had befallen me since I had arrived there at his house.

An icon is a religious representation, sometimes painted on wood or on a wall, and sometimes formed in a mosaic of stone. Those Blackwood took me to examine in a neighbouring room were painted on wood. Icons have a superficial similarity to the stained-glass windows of Western churches and to the paintings of Western artists. But not in less simple, less obvious ways. Icons were actively worshipped as venerated objects. They took on, in a displaced way, the scenes they represented, which became real scenes to the viewers. You did not look on an iconic representation of the crucifixion as a picture seen centuries later, but as the actual crucifixion itself. You yourself lived the scene. The next thing is that icons were highly symbolic, with a symbolism the viewer was expected to understand. The symbols were put together by the artist to tell a story from the New Testament, to depict a church feast, or to show the life of a popular saint. Illiterate people derived religious instruction from looking at them, not from seeking to read the Bible.

When Blackwood had asked me to 'take a look' at his icons, I knew it would be their symbolic meanings in which he would be interested, not the artistic merit of the icons in the Western sense. In fact, judged in a Western sense, the artistic merit of icons is not usually high, and for my part I can either take them or leave them.

Not so Blackwood. He had an evident passion for icons, and he knew far more about them than I did. But, thanks to my attendance at Professor Ortov's lectures on the art forms of Byzantium, at least I was able to hold a reasonably informed conversation with my eccentric host, and to suggest a few opinions. More relevant to me, however, the scene in the bedroom, with the dripping radiator and with the suit laid out on the bed, had itself been an icon of a curious kind, demanding of me that I should read its symbolism. Oddly enough, by the time we finished chattering about the icons, Blackwood and I understood each other better than if we'd presented a fistful of identification cards to each other.

"I'm having a few people in to dinner tonight," he said, as we returned to the book-lined room with the wood fire.

"Artists and archaeologists?"

"Not wholly. There will even be several Outlanders. Scotch?"

He held up a large glass in my direction.

"Thanks, but with ice and plenty of water, please."

So I had moved up on to the red-carpet level, as I'd

begun to suspect, away from the covert activities of Dolfuss, Edelstam, and my father, the red-carpet life I'd always envied so much.

"Anyone in particular that I should meet?" I asked, taking a sip of my drink.

"Oh, you'll find them all interesting."

From this reply I knew that Ralph Blackwood was not my real contact. He was a specialist in his own way, an urbane host given to bringing individuals together. But what took place when they were brought together was not his business. He was as empty of real information as Dolfuss had been.

Someone among the guests that night would be the person I was looking for. It would be for the other person and myself to make our own contact. By now I was beginning to understand something of the methods used by the Outlanders. But, because I was accustomed by my upbringing to human thought processes, the system of the Outlanders still seemed strange to me.

Among the early arrivals was a striking-looking woman, introduced to me as Helga Johnson. She was slightly taller than I was, six feet two or so, and she wore a long dress which enhanced her height even more. She had a mane of blond hair and her eyes were very blue. I judged her to be about ten years older than I was. A dangerous woman, I thought, especially when she gave me a somewhat knowing smile, saying, "I understand I shall be seeing quite a lot of you."

I couldn't see how she could understand anything of the sort, but I left it at that.

I counted sixteen of them, moving in twos and threes, casually and easily, into my icon-loving host's dining room. Two of the walls indeed had been formed into mosaics, not new mosaics but reassembled from stones transferred from some archaeological site. A third wall was decorated by more examples of ancient fine jewellery, while the fourth wall opened into the adjacent area where we had just been chatting.

It was hard to guess who were Outlanders and who were not. I had a feeling that two of the men, both apparently in their mid-thirties, might be. One had been introduced as an engineer, the other as a chemist. My immediate neighbors at the dining table were both red-headed, both women of middle age. There was also a red-headed fellow seated on the opposite side of the table, three places to my right. He had a brown face with strongly marked features. This fellow I knew must be my contact. Three redheads in one dinner party would otherwise be too many. Reflecting that Ralph Blackwood certainly had a peculiar sense of symbolism, or of humour, I gave my attention to conversations with my immediate female neighbours, one of whom turned out to be an archaeologist, and the other a plain housewife, as she called herself. The plain housewife had twinkling blue eyes, which did not belie a keen sense of humour. I had a feeling that I would rather have been assigned to see quite a lot of this plain housewife than of the statuesque Miss Johnson, seated several places to my left at the end of the table.

The dinner itself was something of a shock. My diet had never been of the haute cuisine class. At best it had been simple, at worst frightful, particularly in my student years of feeding at university canteens, especially the one in Moscow. I made no attempt to identify the dishes which now appeared from time to time, carried by servants from some distant kitchen, through the open area where we had foregathered before dinner. I was content just to eat them, thinking it was great to have this kind of food once in a while. But how long would my sharp appetite last if I fed this way every day, as Ralph Blackwood presumably did? I doubted if he enjoyed the dinner as much as I did.

Eventually the ladies retired and we men all moved towards our host at the right-hand end of the table. Some of them cut the ends of cigars, others poured the wine of their choice into sparklingly clean glasses, others cracked nuts, while still others contented themselves with broaching pieces of fruit.

I was a little mortified that of the fourteen, Blackwood and myself apart, I had only been able to identify two Outlanders, the red-headed man and Miss Helga Johnson. Throughout the dinner I had looked vainly for further symbolic indications, and now I listened to the conversations which rippled around me in the hope of enlightenment. There was talk of the world's energy problems, a sensitive subject no doubt, but one which might have arisen anywhere, in thousands of other places. Yet I had the impression of a stage being set, as if this conversation were a bit of the décor being shifted into place.

The butler appeared with a whispered word for our host, who rose immediately, saying, "Well, then, shall we join the ladies?"

At the same instant I caught the eye of the red-headed man. I made the merest nod and he came easily toward me.

"I hear you've been advising Ralph on some of his latest acquisitions," he remarked in a casual voice.

"Hardly that. He knows quite a bit more about it all than I ever will."

"Than I ever will too." The man nodded. We lounged along an adjoining corridor, as if on our way to rejoin the ladies. With a seeming inevitability our short stroll took us to the library, where the fire was burning brightly, as if our arrival there had been anticipated.

"Within a few days you will be taking the first stage," my new friend remarked.

"Where would that be?"

"Mars, of course" was the casual answer.

"Anything I need to know about the trip?"

"Indeed, yes. That's the reason for our little chat."

We sat beside the fire, hunched into large soft chairs. I was glad to be at last at the threshold of a little chat.

"There will be quite a few of you on the trip. You see we've called an energy conference."

"On Mars?"

"Yes. Holding it on Mars will give the Earth representatives a bit of a shock. Bring them closer to reality."

"Who are the Earth representatives to be?"

"Ministers and their officials."

"I'll be travelling with them?"

"Right."

I thought about this for a moment. It would make my position much easier, assuming I was attached officially to the party.

"Will I be attached officially?" I asked.

"That is the idea."

No need then for any more of the cloak-and-dagger stuff. Even so, I felt it would not be a bad idea to have a case prepared against the Earth representatives. I said so.

"Wouldn't it be a good idea really to cut off the power beams? Instead of simply talking about it. Bring them still closer to reality."

"At first sight, you might think so. But it's not quite as simple as that."

"Why not?"

My companion eased himself in the big chair, and then stretched out his legs towards the fire.

"Because we have much less leverage than you might think." This still told me very little.

"I'd have thought we've got enormous leverage. Just cut the power beams off."

"Which would bring on the very chaos we've been at such pains to avoid."

I put two or three chunks of wood on the fire, to give me a few seconds to think this over.

"You see our dilemma?" the redhead went on. "Our only threat is more apparent than real. Yet we still have to convince the Earth people of its reality. Otherwise there'd be chaos, for a different reason of course."

"There'd be endless dissension and fighting, I suppose, among the Earth people. Just as there used to be." I nodded.

"Maybe you understand now why things are the way they are?"

"I'm not sure I do."

"How's that?"

After prodding the fire, I went on hesitantly, searching for words to express my somewhat confused thoughts.

"You know, there's a lot to be said for a pretty tough stance. The way to convince Earth people that the power beams might be stopped is first to convince yourself. I mean convince yourself that you're really going to stop them. Quit fooling around."

"I'm glad you take that point of view."

"Why?"

"Well, you'll be travelling to Mars with the Earth party, don't forget."

"I won't find it difficult to take a strong line, if that's what you mean."

"That's what I do mean."

"But it's not much good me taking a strong line, if a strong line isn't backed up, is it?" I objected.

"Of course it is. Because it's all a matter of psychology."

"Game of bluff?"

"That's right, a game of bluff."

"My opinion, for what it's worth, is that actually cutting the power beams, if only for a month or two, would be worth more than any quantity of bluff."

"It may come to that."

"Not too soon, I'd say." I jabbed once more at the fire.

"We must try negotiation first. But it won't do any harm to have you throwing a scare or two into them."

"Who," I said slowly, "will finally decide all this?"

The redhead rose from his chair. I caught a flash from his eyes, enhanced by the firelight, so that it seemed more like a warning than a gesture.

"You have all the information you need," he said, in a voice curiously reminiscent of my father. The unexpected association caused me to falter for the short time we took to leave the library. Indeed, by the time I'd recovered my wits, we were on our way to 'join the ladies.' There was a loud buzz of conversation ahead as we walked the corridor from the library, which caused me to bite back the final questions that were running in my mind. Which was how much of it this red-headed fellow really knew. Did he know something of the larger pattern? Or was he a specialist also, like Dolfuss and Blackwood, limited to only a particular facet of the whole thing? I found it hard to let him go without seeking some indication of the answers to these questions. But go he did, helter-skelter, as if I'd said

113

something unbelievably repelling in its content.

Soon thereafter I found myself wedged in a corner by the powerful Miss Johnson. I became acutely conscious of the muscles of her back and shoulders, clearly revealed by the dress she was wearing. As she talked I kept wondering just how strong she really was, to the point where I had an irrational desire to put the matter to test, there and then, in front of the whole company.

"I'll send a car for you tomorrow, in the mid-morning," she said. "The sooner we have you aboard, the better."

"Good." I nodded. "Less chance for something to go amiss."

"What should go amiss?"

"Oh, I might fall into a crevasse, I suppose."

I watched her grey eyes for a reaction to this, but there was none. From which I concluded that she knew nothing of my crossing of the pass. She was from the launching station on the Anatolian plateau, still another specialist, it seemed.

It had been a strange day, I reflected as I lay in bed that night. Beginning at the Dolfuss hideaway in the remote countryside, it was ending in an elegant bedroom of an elegant town house, following an elegant dinner with elegant people. So strange in fact that I'd almost expected to find Helga Johnson waiting there in the bedroom, anxious to put her powerfully muscled shoulders to the test. There was a less light-hearted side to it, however.

During the days I'd spent with Dolfuss and with Lena —Lena whom I knew I was destined to remember always with a sharp stab of regret—I'd more or less taken it for granted that I'd be smuggled into the Anatolian space station, smuggled in Dolfuss's own particular style, disguised as a pig or something. Since Dolfuss plainly had his own way of doing things, I'd more or less left it at that. Now, in the few minutes before I fell asleep, I could see there would be problems with this line of approach. Getting a person from a special inner place into a general outside freedom was a different kind of operation from the reverse. Getting a person from outside into a special inside place was something needing a quite separate form of organization. That this second form of operation was Ralph Blackwood's job I'd no doubt. But how the devil he was going to do it, remembering the electronic and the computerized surveillance that would have to be defeated, I couldn't see at all.

The moment I awoke the following morning I had the beginning of an answer. I was aware, as I came out of the mists of sleep, of a movement in the room, and then of a faint click as the outer door was closed. Rolling immediately off the bed, I saw that a breakfast tray had been delivered. On it were a jug of coffee, rolls, butter, and honey, and a sealed plain white envelope. In the envelope was a square piece of an orange-coloured material, on one side of which were a number of miniaturized printed circuits. Inlaid on the other side, with its fastenings in titanium metal, was a photograph of myself. Immediately above the photograph, the orange-coloured material was perforated by two rows of punched holes.

Also inside the envelope was a typed note, which read:

Your car will leave promptly at 11 A.M.
R. Blackwood

I ate the breakfast, shaved, took a shower, and dressed in the suit I'd used on the previous evening. Although the white envelope with its curious contents was somewhat large, I found it fitted neatly into an inner pocket of the jacket, as if the pocket had been constructed with exactly this intention.

Since it was still only 9.30 A.M., I felt I had ample time to put a question or two to my host. But after prowling through the less private rooms of the house, and not finding Ralph Blackwood anywhere there, I began to wonder. At length I came on the butler.

"I'd like to have a word with Mr. Blackwood," I said, "to thank him for his kindness."

"I will be glad to convey your message, sir," the butler replied without the slightest flicker.

"Ah, so Mr. Blackwood isn't available?"

"He had to go into the city, sir. Unexpectedly."

"Then please do convey my thanks and my regards. By the way, where does the car leave from?"

"The front of the house, sir. Perhaps you'd like to see the papers while you wait?"

"Well, if it's not too much of an imposition, what I'd really like to do would be to take another look at Mr. Blackwood's new icons."

"Oh, certainly, sir. If you'll just follow me."

Actually, I'd no particular wish to see the icons again, but at least they would be as interesting as the morning papers. Besides, I wanted to leave Ralph Blackwood with a slight taste of the unusual. With a bit of luck he might even get the idea that the icons had a special significance for me. Perhaps indeed they might contain an inner message which would now be revealed to me?

But if they did I couldn't find it. Truth to tell, I was more concerned with the peculiarities of Mr. Blackwood himself than I was with the icons. His speciality seemed to lie in avoiding overt contact with his contacts. In place of the clandestine whispers of a normal agent he substituted signs and symbols. Any direct mention of his activities, like discussing the questions I'd wanted to put to him, would I now felt sure have brought an expression of intense distaste to his finely-modelled face. Rather than admit to any involvement, I felt sure he would prefer to run a mile, which of course was just what he had done.

I was jerked from these thoughts by a touch on the arm. It was the butler again,

"The car is here, sir."

"Oh, thank you. The icons were interesting. I'd be grateful if you'd tell Mr. Blackwood that the second one from the left contains a most unusual symbol."

There was cherry blossom in flower as the car sped in a zigzag course through suburban avenues. Within half an hour the driver and I (for there was no one else in the car) approached a broad highway. Immediately before reaching it, my driver brought the car to a stop, and then set himself back with the evident intention of waiting. I tried to ask the reason for the delay, but the driver's rapidly spoken Turkish went beyond my minuscule comprehension of the language. So we just waited there, I in the back of Blackwood's sumptuous limousine.

Perhaps ten minutes later, a stream of about ten other large cars, with a motorcycle police escort, came along the main highway from the direction of the city centre. My driver started his engine, revved it for a moment, sounded his horn loudly, and turned out into the highway, with the evident intention of joining the cavalcade. This was made easy for him by the driver of one of the other cars, who stopped in order to allow ours to pull ahead of him.

By now, two of the motorcycle cops had pulled up alongside us. My driver explained something to them. For answer, one of the cops came to my window. "Pass?" was his brusque request. I slipped the orange-colored electronic card from my pocket. The cop took a look at my picture, and then, satisfied apparently, returned to his bike.

At that point, a woman got out of the car behind, the one which had stopped to allow us into the highway. "Here we go again," I thought to myself, for the woman was Helga Johnson. She walked majestically toward us, poking her head inside the window on my right, saying without apparent recognition, "I wonder if we could transfer a passenger. We're a bit crowded in our car."

"Of course," I agreed, whereon she turned to the two cops, explaining that a passenger from her car would move into mine. The second cop strolled to the car behind. After taking a quick look inside it, he nodded agreement, whereon Helga Johnson escorted a man of about fifty-five, wearing a dark suit and dark hat, from her car to mine. If the idea was to expose me to this fellow, or to expose him to me, the manoeuvre seemed a bit crude, rather unworthy of Mr. Ralph Blackwood, I thought.

The man turned out to be from the Western Energy Authority. After we had introduced ourselves, he asked, "Who are you representing?"

"The Outlanders," I answered, not seeing any advantage in dissembling.

Instantly the fellow went cold. "Thought you were a bit young to be one of us," he muttered.

Thereafter he fell silent, obviously concluding that I'd been set up to pump him. Thinking that indeed I had been set up to pump him of something, I grinned as disarmingly as I could manage, in view of my still malevolent left eye, and said, "Well, you know, if I was looking for an indiscretion I'd hardly have told you I was an Outlander, would I?"

This registered. After a moment, he relaxed a bit.

"The trouble is you look like one of us," he remarked.

"I might say the same."

"Disturbing, though."

"Never know who you're dealing with?"

"That's right."

By now I was having doubts about the pumping theory. Not only was the passenger-swap device too crude, but this fellow didn't seem promising material to me. In fact, as I listened to his maunderings, I began to wish I'd given a cold reception to Helga Johnson's request. I had more interesting things to concern me, like what the hell was going on. I was not the smallest step further in answering the question of how all the planning by the Outlanders was arranged. Who gave the instructions to Dolfuss, to Ralph Blackwood, to the red-headed man at yesterday's dinner, or to my father for that matter? And what had my father meant by saying that it was necessary for him to keep faith with the dead? None of it made any sense to me, and yet somehow there had to be sense in it somewhere.

The journey was a long one. The party stopped for lunch at an hotel overlooking a large lake, which was said to have yielded the fish we ate. I mixed freely with the party, making no attempt to seek out Helga Johnson, or to hang on to the coattails of my fellow passenger. However, because the party seemed mostly to know each other, I never got into any meaningful conversation, my remarks being all of the "will you please pass the salt" variety. Wine flowed pretty freely, increasing the noise volume, which also made ordered discussion still more difficult, to a point where I decided not to bother myself any further.

Back in the car, I nodded as my companion appeared. "A bit strange we didn't come by helicopter," I remarked, by way of something to say. A surprised look flitted across the fellow's face, "Oh," he replied, "I thought it was because you Outlanders object to helicopters being used near your base." Since this remark gave him a point of advantage, it gave me the opportunity to fall silent.

The country ahead was rising steadily, implying that we were approaching the general area of the plateau, if not our actual destination itself. Hour after hour we gained height, until at last the road ahead was barred by a vast steel construction, through which there were two massive gates.

"Looks like the main security checkpoint," I said, in a more cheerful voice than I felt.

"You Outlanders certainly take a lot of trouble to stop people." My companion's voice had an anxious note to it. His implication, that this was an Outlander checkpoint, might well be true, but I felt certain it was also used by world governments. It was a kind of frontier, no doubt with both sides on the watch.

My companion took an orange-coloured card from his briefcase. Outwardly it was just like the one which had come to me on my breakfast tray.

"I expect they'll be wanting these," he said.

"I wouldn't be surprised," I replied, making no move to get out my own card.

"I wonder if they'll be wanting us out of the car?" There was a detectably nervous inflexion in the voice now.

A body of officials moved toward the cavalcade, two of them to each car. The two allotted to our car came together, first to my window. By now I had my orange-coloured electronic pass in my hand, using it to screen my face. Once the two chaps were close alongside, I allowed myself to come forward a bit towards them. They both compared the photograph with me. Satisfied of the likeness, they withdrew to the other side of the car, where my companion was subjected to the same process. Then they both withdrew, taking our passes with them. As we waited, for perhaps twenty minutes, I kept glancing at the fellow beside me. The slight involuntary tensing of the fingers showed him to be under stress. I knew now why Helga Johnson had manoeuvred him into my car. If either one of us was to be stopped here, it would surely be he. A child could have spotted the wretched man. But spotted he was not. The guards eventually returned our passes, the steel gates were opened, smoothly without sound so far as I could detect, and one by one the cars passed through to the far side, into the space station controlled by the Outlanders.

"Did you say you were a scientist?" I asked, once we were well clear of the barrier.

The chap seemed to jump a mile up into the air. "Oh, no! I'm in the administration division."

I could only think he must be an extremely good scientist, for he was a singularly inept agent. His reply had told me all I wanted to know.

My treatment at the hands of the two main intelligence agencies, at the pleasant-looking house in the pleasant-looking street, now put world governments in a distinctly delicate position so far as their negotiations with the Outlanders were concerned. So much so that strenuous efforts would surely have been made to stop me at the barrier if it had been known that I was still alive. But world governments, unfortunately for them, thought I had literally gone up in smoke, cremated.

Even so, passage through the barrier had been by no means straightforward. The pass I'd been given clearly had an electronic code-marking for the operation itself. But it also had an electronic representation of the physical characteristics of its bearer, which had surely been fed into a terminal linked to distant high-speed, high-storage computers. Those characteristics had already been compared with data in a central bank possessed by world governments, and presumably also in a data bank possessed by the Outlanders. This had been done by the time the guards had returned to the cars. If my own characteristics had actually been entered electronically on my pass, their discovery would have come as an unpleasant shock to world governments. Agencies would have been contacted. After some delay for consultations, I would surely have been arrested—or a diplomatic reason would more likely have been offered for holding me back at the barrier. It therefore followed that the characteristics entered electronically on my pass were not my own.

How were the guards to cope with this deception? Through the photographs on the passes, which they had carefully compared with the persons carrying the passes. Yet there still remained one loophole for duplicity, either by world governments or by the Outlanders. The electronic representation need not match the photograph. The way to close out this loophole would have been for us all to have paraded in front of a television camera, the output from which could have been checked against the electronic representation on the pass. It was indeed my recognition of this acid test which had troubled me from the moment I'd received the pass that morning on my breakfast tray.

One objection to such a test's being made was that the high-level persons who formed our present party might well have objected to it. But I had been worried that this objection would not prove strong enough. Another factor —as it turned out the crucial one—was that both sides might want to cheat in the same way. My neighbour's pass was just as dubious as my own, and in the same way. The difference had been that the Outlanders knew perfectly well they were being cheated, and had made use of the fact, whereas world governments had been unaware of it. Almost certainly there had been a mutual agreement not to use television cameras. But to guard against this agreement's being broken by world governments, Helga Johnson had arranged the transfer of the scientist chap to my car, so making sure that whatever cameras there might have been would be kept well clear of us. Even so, I'd taken good care to keep my face well away from the car window, to avoid even a slight risk.

At all events, I was now inside the barrier. It was to prove the entry to a radically new phase of my life, just as I expected it to be.

Farewell, Earth! I looked at the scanner screen, which showed the beautiful planet that was all the home I had ever known. The 'home' of the Outlanders was but a concept in my mind, not to compare emotionally with the splendidly coloured vision which now swam before my tear-filled eyes. The winter snows of the Idaho woods and hills were somewhere there, hidden beneath a vast canopy of cloud which covered the whole of the northern Rockies. I would never see them again, never ski again down bright sunlit slopes, never set my foot in the new grass of a spring meadow, never breathe free air again into my lungs. These were my convictions as I gazed endlessly, hour by hour, at the receding vision of the Earth. Deep within me I also had a conviction that I would soon be learning things that were alien to my human style of thinking, things that I would find infinitely repulsive in their content.

Meanwhile there were lesser problems, for instance the problem of Helga Johnson. She appeared to be the medical officer assigned to the party. At any rate she had gone round administering a shot of something or other immediately before blast-off, which had taken place an hour before dawn, the day following our car journey from Ankara. The shot was supposed to protect us against heart failure during the minute or so of powerful acceleration at the beginning. Whether it did or not I couldn't tell, but at least we had no fatalities on our hands.

I knew this because once a day the whole party assembled for a meal, which enabled me to keep tabs on everybody. We sat at two long tables, with members of the crew at the ends. We kept to our usual twenty-four-hour cycle, so that we all tended to think of these meals as 'dinner,' although by now there was no connexion for us between the twenty-four-hour cycle and the rising and setting of the Sun—the Sun was always there in the scanner, at all times.

I soon saw that the purpose of the meals was to keep us all locked in the twenty-four-hour cycle, and also to keep us all phased in the same way with respect to it. Which I suppose was useful to the crew, because it meant that we all tended to sleep during the same hours. The crew members changed from day to day, which made it hard to get to know them, particularly as changing places at the table were assigned to us from day to day. This had the advantage of shuffling us around constantly, preventing the party from coagulating into a few self-contained cliques. But it also meant that one sat next to a crew member only rarely, and to a different one each time.

I had a cabin to myself, in which I found a stack of writing paper. Whether or not this was intended as a 'sign,' in the manner of Ralph Blackwood, it was during the one-month journey to Mars that I set down the bulk of my story, beginning not at the beginning but with a description of my treatment at the hands of the intelligence agencies. This I felt might be important for the Outlanders, and indeed I had reason to believe that my writing on this matter was noted and copied, for during the hour of dinner my written sheets of paper were disturbed on at least two occasions. With the intelligence agency episode thus described, I then added the earlier and later parts, coming eventually up to date at the current moment.

Unlike the other crew members, who remain shadowy figures in my mind, there was one of whom I saw plenty. This was Helga Johnson. She had a key to my cabin, and as she'd promised on the evening of the dinner at Ralph Blackwood's house, she was forever in and out of the cabin.

Our relationship was not of affection, such as I might have felt for Lena, the sometime desk clerk in the Moscow University bookstore. It was a far more primeval business. The same desire I'd felt on the first evening, to test the strength of the rippling muscles of her shoulders and back, returned. To my senses she seemed to flaunt herself unbearably. It was not long therefore before we had

125

begun to wrestle, at first half playfully, and then in seriousness. As I have just said, the relationship had little affection in it. My ungallant aim was to reduce the woman to a state of gasping helplessness. It was an end she resisted with animal ferocity, but which she was plainly anxious to achieve. When it was over we both lay exhausted, side by side. Then Helga Johnson stood up and slowly withdrew from my cabin, significantly without any softening smile flickering for even a moment across her face.

Yet Helga Johnson it was who showed me something of the greatest importance. She took me one day on a tour of the ship. My first surprise was to find that through most of the ship the downward pull on the body was only about a third of terrestrial gravity, whereas in the more limited parts of the ship, where my party were accustomed to dining, and where our cabins were, the downward pull was much the same as terrestrial gravity. I decided this must be a concession to our special passenger status, for while it was easy enough merely to move under the low pull, I found it much harder to control myself in a precise way. In fact, I stumbled badly in attempting to follow behind Helga Johnson, who was evidently well used to the different conditions.

She led me to a kind of control bridge where there was a scanner screen different in its viewing angles from the one I was accustomed to, which pointed mainly backward towards the Earth. This one pointed ahead, into a star-filled background.

"Look!" my companion exclaimed. "Can you see those two streaks of light." It wasn't easy to distinguish the streaks from the fiery arch of the Milky Way, but once I had them I could find them more easily the second time.

"Know what they are?" she continued.

"No," I admitted, as a crew member appeared beside us.

"They're the laser beams supplying power to the Earth," the crew member broke in.

"They're much fainter than I expected."

The crew member chuckled. "They wouldn't be faint if you were in one of 'em," he said, grinning. "In fact, you'd be fried instantly to a crisp. We see those streaks only because of the exceedingly small quantity of gas in space, through which the beams are shining."

"Like shafts of sunlight picking out bits of dust?"

"The same sort of thing."

So here at last were the power beams, the beams along which Earth received its energy supply from the Outlanders. The beams themselves were directed from the region of Jupiter toward the Sun, but up out of the plane of the orbit of Jupiter, at an angle of about fifteen degrees, so they were never intercepted by a planet, satellite, or asteroid. After propagating inwards, they were then reflected, in some complex manner, directly towards Earth, one beam passing under the control of the Western powers, the other to the East. Interruption of these beams would spell disaster for the teeming billions of people on the Earth. It was just this that my story had been all about. It was this that would be discussed at the forthcoming meeting on the planet Mars. It was this that was supposed to give the Outlanders their control over Earth people.

Nuclear research by Earth scientists had for long been forbidden, since the discovery of an effective system of nuclear fusion would permit Earth to escape from this control. Yet the prohibition was known to be only partial, with both West and East seeking to cheat whenever they could. No doubt my scientist-companion on the car journey from Ankara had come on this trip in the hope of acquiring items of essential information. No doubt also it had been in the monitoring and control of Earth activities that my father had been largely employed. According to my red-headed friend at the house of Ralph Blackwood, it was the political aim of the Outlanders to maintain control over the Earth, without ever going to the extreme step of actually cutting out these beams. Personally, I was sceptical of this restrained policy. My own recommendation would be to hit hard, and to keep on hitting hard. But this I had to admit was an opinion based on my habit of thinking like a human. Plainly, the Outlanders formulated their plans in a more subtle way, with a defter handling of the psychological make-up of their opponents.

But there was nothing subtle about Helga Johnson, except in having inveigled me into the part of the ship where the downward pull was so much reduced. There came a time in our tour of the ship when we arrived at her own quarters. I realised just where we were at the moment a door clicked behind me, before she said, "And now, little man, the advantage is with me."

Not that I was more than a fraction less tall than she was, but she somehow contrived to make me feel small. There was a singular look in the grey eyes, which I suppose I might describe as lust. The whole blazing, furious aspect of the woman went outside my experience.

I soon found myself unable to cope. She was far more skilful in gaining purchase for those muscled arms and legs than I was. I was always scrambling for something firm to push against, usually without effect. I suppose I could have stuck my fingers hard into her eyes but I had no wish to blind the woman, much as I would have been glad to make her howl otherwise. She evidently greatly savoured her revenge, and it was my turn at last to withdraw without a smile.

Thereafter, for the rest of the voyage, Helga Johnson and I fought an unremitting sexual battle. There were no more impromptu visits to my cabin, because there, in a region of stronger pull, I had the advantage. Equally, I avoided parts of the ship where the downward pull was weak. This meant that our regular meetings were restricted to the daily meals, at which we would shamelessly seek to excite each other, in spite of the presence of the staid party of Earthlanders. The route to success for me lay in a steadfast determination that I would return directly to my own cabin—precisely the opposite I noted from the usual troubadour convention. Provided I maintained this determination for two or three days on end, Helga Johnson's restraint would give way, and she would follow, eventually giving me the opportunity to trap her and force her into my cabin, in a manner absurdly reminiscent of the caveman with his club. My now inevitable victories on those occasions would then convince me that I could overcome the woman even on her own ground. In fact, this became my ambition, to win both ways, as I think it was also her ambition. But neither of us ever succeeded.

Events always come as an unexpected surprise for the perennial sucker, which I had long since become. Nobody can be blamed for not foreseeing a truly unusual situation. It is when subtle indications of what is to happen are always blandly ignored that you qualify as the real sucker, the way it always seemed to be happening with me. I'd been convinced that I was travelling to Mars for a high-level Outlanders versus Earthlanders confrontation, in

129

which I held some quite important cards. But it didn't turn out that way, and in retrospect I can see I should have been forewarned. There had been more than enough signs and symbols, as I'm sure my erstwhile host Mr. Ralph Blackwood would not have been at a loss to point out.

The truth of it was that already during the journey from Earth to Mars the party of ministers and their advisers had become a charade. A charade for me, that is to say. For themselves, there were frequent discussions, and much nodding and winking at this, that, and the other. I'd seen it all going on around me, and yet I'd had no urge to plunge into it, as I would have had if the thought of the Martian conference had moved me to any important degree. Instead, I'd become absorbed in my writing, in my own thoughts, and of course in my own particular charade with Helga Johnson. By now I'd come to suspect a subtle psychological plan in everything, so much so that I can't help wondering if my distraction with the tumultuous Helga wasn't also a part of some plan, a plan to tide me over the journey in an inconsequential fashion, occupying me intensely for the while, but not leaving any deeply lasting impressions, no scars in the memory.

The Martian landing was an easy affair, giving us much less of a pounding than the take-off from Earth had done. Thereafter the downward pull on my body decreased slowly to Martian gravity, implying that the rotary movement within the ship, which had been responsible before for the pull, had now been shut down. I found my cabin door locked, from which I deduced that under the reduced pull Helga Johnson was going to have one final fling at me. But in this I was wrong again. Eventually there was a metallic click, the cabin door swung open, and on the threshold stood a figure the like of whom I could not have foreseen, even in the wildest flight of my imagination.

The little fellow who stood there was dressed in an outrageous combination of mauve pants and bright yellow singlet. He wore a small white pork-pie hat, with a brown pigtail of hair hanging almost to the waist. He came forward,

"Aye, tha'll be t'chap," he said with a broad wink.

"I'll be what?"

"T'chap I'm to fetch. To Macro's ship."

This was the first indication of things being different, but it was delivered in so curious a fashion that I disdained to believe it.

"I'm not going to anybody's ship. I'm here for a conference between the Outlanders and the Earthlanders."

At this, the fellow gave a crow-like laugh.

"Conference my eye," he croaked, "at least conference your eye. They told me to fetch t'chap wi't eye. You got it, maister. A regular evil eye it is. If you're not this eye chap, who is, I'd like ta knaw?"

"Who told you?"

"Never thee mind. Sithe, just coom along. And be nippy abaht it."

"Who might I be . . ."

Again there was the death's-head laugh.

"Na then," went on the little man, "doan't give me that stuff. Cos I doan't tak to it. Sam Ossett's the name."

"O.K., Sam," I said, shaking his outstretched hand. My recent bouts with Helga Johnson must have made my grip a bit above the vigorous.

"Bloomin' 'eck," yelped the little man, "what dost tak me for, a joiner's vise?"

"Sorry, Sam." I grinned as I slackened off immediately. "You one of these Outlanders?"

"Outlanders or Earthlanders, they're all t'same to me. Ah coom fro' Yorkshire" was the astonishing reply.

Then, with a flick of his pigtail, Sam went on, "Got onny bags?"

I had only my writing, a few odds and ends, and a pile of underclothes I'd taken from the room in Ralph Blackwood's house.

"Who is this Macro?" I asked as we quitted the cabin.

"Tha'll know 'im when tha sees 'im" was the cryptic reply.

Whatever Sam's other deficiencies he certainly knew his way around the vast complex of Martian buildings which had been built into the smooth, gently rising slopes of Olympus Mons. I was able to gaze out of vast windows at the dust-lashed scene outside, thinking it must have been quite a problem to find window material that would not be hopelessly scored by the fiercely blown streams of dust that were hitting them. I could not help reflecting on the paradox of a technology which was capable of erecting a planetary base of this kind and which yet permitted elementary defects, like bad plumbing and elevators that wouldn't work. The buildings I knew to be anchored by piles driven deeply into the hard-frozen ice and volcanic ash which formed most of the uplifted structure of Olympus Mons.

For all his small size, Sam Ossett was able to scurry along at a great pace, so that it was all I could do to keep up with him, especially as he never gave me warning of the twists and turns which lay along our route through the buildings, with their halls, chutes, and corridors. Occasionally, I managed to get out a question, which was hardly ever answered in intelligible terms. However, to the most important question, "Where is this ship of Macro's heading to?" he gave his wheezing cackle, and then added, "Inta t'outer regions. Where else would it be goin'?"

"Towards Jupiter?"

"Aye, ta Jupiter. Didn't ah say t'outer regions? Eh then?"

So I padded along beside my eccentric guide, wondering why I should put the slightest trust in him, or in this Macro fellow. He had offered no credentials, but were there ever credentials that one could really believe? The orange-coloured pass which had enabled me to quit the Earth had seemed magnificently official, and yet it had been phoney. Anything could be phoney, except perhaps one's own instinct. My instinct about Sam Ossett was that he was just too peculiar to be phoney. I felt that neither Western nor Eastern Intelligence could possibly have had the imagination to invent such a creature. The limit of their perception would have been to send a man from Princeton, or from an English public school.

As if in reply to my thoughts, Sam stopped suddenly. He swung his pigtail again, adjusted his pork-pie hat, and said, "Aye. Tha's a reight evil-lookin' chap. Ah doan't know ah'm goin' to feel easy travellin' wi't likes o' thee."

Then without waiting for a reply he resumed his scurrying progress through the labyrinthian structure of the Martian station.

We arrived at length at what was clearly a disembarkment hall, although to me it looked more like an unusually large basketball court. The reason for my illusion was the dozen or so men assembled there. Without exception, they all topped seven feet in height. One among them, stripped to the waist so that I could see huge muscles rippling everywhere over his arms, shoulders, and torso, stepped forward as we approached.

"I am Macro," he announced in the bass voice of an ancient patriarch.

Thinking that here was the true mate for Helga Johnson, I was careful to make a slight bow rather than to offer my hand.

"Glad to know you," I half grunted. Of course it made good sense, there under conditions of weak gravity, to have these huge men. But then what was the shrivelled figure of Sam Ossett doing among them?

"When do we leave?" I continued.

"As soon as we have you aboard." Macro's reply was in a kind of space-pidgen language, with a singsong lilt to it, which I cannot hope to render in a literal fashion.

"Then we'll go aboard right away." I nodded.

For answer, Macro stepped up on a dais at one side of the hall. He lifted his arms and began to speak. As he did so, other men of enormous stature began immediately to enter the hall. I tried to figure out what he was saying, but Sam Ossett plucked my sleeve.

"Sithe," he hissed, "ah doan't want us to get trodden on." He pulled me along with him, into a tunnel which led us after about two hundred paces into the ship itself.

So, after this flurry of activity, taking I suppose about two hours, I found myself in a new cabin in a new ship. The cabin was less soft in its furnishings than the first one had been, but it had its own scanning screen, which was a clear advantage. Also it had means to prepare food, from which I guessed there would be no daily meetings for dinner as there had been before. Indeed the nature of the cabin suggested that I would be expected to stay there, rather than to be always roaming over the whole ship. This first impression proved to be correct, for as I discovered later, the ship, while fast, was not large, much of its interior being given over to technical facilities. Personal facilities were thus at a premium, and since mine were more spacious than those afforded to the huge crewmen, I naturally was expected to stick closely by them. In short, it would be only on rare occasions that I would quit the comparative comfort of my cabin for the more austere conditions which existed in other parts of the ship.

Once he had deposited me in the cabin, Sam Ossett left without a further word. Like the landing, blast-off from Mars was a comparatively gentle affair. It came several hours later, which I supposed to have been taken up in final checks and adjustments of a technical nature. Nobody ever seemed capable of getting a ship out into space at a moment's notice.

I now had a great view of the surface of Mars, which had been denied me during the landing. Great, in an awe-inspiring way. Craters, enormous canyons, storm-streaked plains, volcanic uplands like the one where the station lay combined into a scene that was both desolate and magnificent.

I found the scanning screen could be turned to view any part of the heavens, except for a close proximity to the Sun, which I guessed to be a safety precaution, to prevent the system from burning out. After a search of the heavens I eventually found the planet Jupiter. I knew it from the four large satellites which could be seen in the scanner, and from their motions around Jupiter, which I followed from day to day—I still kept to my twenty-four-hour cycle, although by now it had little relation to any aspect of my environment.

As the days and weeks were to pass by I would follow the slowly-growing image of Jupiter. There was also a growing excitement within me, since at last I was approaching the territory of the Outlanders. Somewhere ahead of me was the elusive 'home' towards which I was now headed. Mixed with the excitement, and tempering it, was my feeling of a dreaded knowledge which I felt myself to be on the verge of understanding. This dread always surged through me whenever I turned the scanner deep into the heart of the Milky Way. As the myriads of stars blazed upon the screen I wondered just what lay out there, what wonders, what peculiarities.

Sam Ossett was right when he said he would be travelling with me. From time to time he appeared in my cabin, always in his white pork-pie hat. I grew desperately anxious to know what lay beneath it, but never in my presence did he so much as lift it for a moment from his head, although he often changed its tilt to suit his mood. One day he pulled out a pack of cards, which he proceeded to riffle in an expert manner.

"Fancy a game?" he asked.

"Sure would," I responded, "but I'm not heeled."

Here Sam pulled out a wallet, from which he proceeded to count out a thousand dollars. Splitting it evenly, and then pushing several notes and a pile of counters in front of me, he returned to shuffling the pack.

"I wouldn't object to being staked, if there was any chance of my paying it back," I said.

Sam gave his by now well-known death's-head croak. "I'm not objectin'," he stated, "'cos I'm going to win it back." Then he tapped me on the knee. "Sithe lad," he went on, "I can sign a check i' seven figures."

Win it back he did. We started on gin rummy. Finding

Sam to be something of an expert, I switched to blackjack. It made no difference. Sam went on winning, because as far as I could tell he simply remembered every card we played. He won in spite of several large bottles of a fiendishly strong beer which he produced.

"Stingo," he explained with satisfaction, as he quaffed a draught of the stuff, reorienting the pork-pie hat but not taking it off.

For the next two months my sole contact with the world outside my cabin was through Sam Ossett. He came to see me two or three times a week, "to see how tha't gettin' on, lad," as he always explained. At each visit he would stake me five hundred dollars, which he always won back again over the next two hours or so.

Two months may sound a long time to be cooped up in a small place, but curiously enough it didn't seem that way. My sense of time became peculiarly contracted, with the twenty-four-hour cycles seeming to go by at an ever-increasing rate. Jupiter became increasingly more menacing on the viewing screen. The laser beams carrying power to the Earth could now be more plainly seen—with the scanner appropriately turned they formed bright lances crossing the whole of the screen.

"Sudden't be long nah," Sam remarked one day.

"What won't be long?"

"Tha't allus wantin' to know, aren't ta?"

"Of course I am. What won't be long?"

"T'end o' course."

I didn't see how this could possibly be the end, because so far as I could tell there was nothing of any significance immediately ahead of the ship. An asteroid possibly, but surely the 'home' of the Outlanders couldn't be located on a small asteroid? As if to distract me from the question,

Sam gave my elbow a tweak. Then after rummaging in a pocket from which he produced a rough cotton bag, he went on, "Somethin' to show tha." So saying he emptied four whitish stones from the bag on to his palm. Although uncut, and not sparkling in an overwhelming way, it wasn't difficult to guess that Sam had got himself a bag of the largest diamonds I'd ever seen, larger indeed than I'd ever heard of.

"I just pick 'em up, on one of these 'ere hasteroids," he said.

"Off the ground?"

"Aye, off t'grund."

Sam handed me one of the stones, which I turned over in my open hand. There was a curiously corrupting feeling about holding a fortune in that way. When I moved to hand it back, he shook his head.

"Keep 'od on it, lad. Don't worry abaht me. There's plenty more where that coom fro'. Didn't ah say ah could sign a cheque i' seven figures?"

"Thanks," I said with a smile. "I'll keep it as a talisman."

"Aye, do that. Tha might need it one fine day." He tapped my knee, and then went on, "Tha knows, I wouldn't be i' thy shoes, lad, not for a bloody fortune I wouldn't." With this Parthian shot he took his leave of my cabin, his pigtail swinging across a shoulder, his hat inclined at a rakish angle—a result of the 'stingo' he had just consumed.

It was not long after this that one of Macro's enormous crewmen came to my cabin. He indicated by signs that I should follow him, which I did. He led me through the crowded complex structure of the rocket, until we came to an open area where Macro himself was standing beside a pile of equipment. He was dressed now in blazoned shirt and trousers, consisting of red and light blue streaks on black, as if to imitate the flashes of lightning across a dark sky.

The equipment consisted mostly of a space suit, into which I was dressed. There were the usual helmet and air supply. But there were also several unusual features whose operation I had difficulty to understand. There was a curious kind of large wrist watch, with a single pointer and a graduated dial ranging from zero to a hundred.

"It is most important," Macro stated in his sing-song voice.

"Why is it important?" I asked.

"Because it must always go the same way" was the seemingly incomprehensible answer.

"The same way?"

"Yes, the same way." Macro indicated the 'same way' by standing at his full height, and then swinging his right arm in a vast circle. "Always the same way," he asserted.

"Always the same way," echoed two nearby crewmen, also swinging their arms in circles in the same mysterious fashion.

"I see," I mused, "always the same way."

"Yes, yes, always the same way," roared Macro and his two men, as if to make an opera out of it.

Then there was a gunlike device.

"Gun. Gun," Macro boomed. Feeling the explanation to be superfluous, I picked the thing up. Directing the barrel toward the floor, I pressed the trigger. There was a faint hissing sound, at which Macro and the others boomed in response, "Gun! Gun!"

"Nah then, what's all this abaht? Eh then?" came the familiar voice of Sam Ossett.

"They're telling me this damn thing is a gun."

"Bleedin' 'eck, what else dost think it is?"

"I thought it might be a sundial, or a broom handle. But what the hell does it *do?*" I asked in exasperation, pressing the trigger and letting the thing make its faint fizz again.

Sam Ossett flicked his pigtail, a manoeuvre which seemed to presage a moment of decision.

"Ee then! Not much of a gun, is it?"

At this, he broke into a strange language, spoken in a voice that ranged fully over three octaves. There was a long and animated reply from Macro, after which Sam turned back to me, saying, "Tha'd nivver credit it, would ta? It's a gun."

"A gun?"

"Aye, a gun. Bloomin' 'eck! But tha'll be needin' to find it aht for thisen. Like?"

"Like what?"

"Like tha'll be findin' it aht for thisen."

At this I gave it up. Bleedin' 'eck.

Actually I did find something out for myself. On several occasions I was called to try on the space suit, to familiarize myself with it. On one of these occasions I discovered that the gun could be neatly fitted into one or other of the gauntlets which covered my hands. Since this discovery came as a surprise to the others, I concluded that they understood as little about the gun as I did.

Then a moment came when Sam Ossett appeared in my cabin for the last time.

"Tha's 'ome, lad," he announced. "No great shakes of a place," he added in his flat, monotonous voice.

I knew from the scanner that we were now close to Jupiter, for the great planet had grown rapidly on the screen until it had become an awesome and daunting object.

"How can I be home in this place?" I asked.

"Nay, doan't ask me. If t'Outlanders are keen to live in this God-forsaken 'ole, then that's their awn business, nut mine, lad."

"Can't you be a bit more helpful?"

"Ee, lad, ah'd not be true to misen, if I was to start chantin' anthems abaht it."

"Well, goodbye, Sam. It's been great knowing you. Remember me to Yorkshire."

"I'll do that, lad. When ah'm sittin' down to mi' glass o' stingo, ah'll think abaht thee, and abaht this place o' thine."

So saying he guided me through the ship to the open area where my suit was waiting ready for me. Macro was there, dressed again in gaudy clothes—he had a different set every time I saw him. Together with a crewman he bundled me into the suit. Their voices came muffled to my ears through the headpiece. Soon I was negotiating an air lock, to find myself emerging into a kind of long bridge which led from the docking area to some inner haven. The bridge was enclosed in translucent material, frosted over with large white crystals, which I could see were not snowflakes.

There was a rail by which I could haul myself without undue difficulty. It brought me eventually to several air locks. I think there were three of them, but my mind was confused, so I cannot be sure of my memory. After each of the locks, I tested for air pressure, in the way that Macro and his crewmen had taught me to do. At the last of them, since the pressure and air composition were satisfactory, I worked my way out of the suit. Only then did I realise I was in an antechamber to a large hall.

I had expected some kind of welcome. At the very least

I had expected to be met by one or more Outlanders. I had expected to arrive at a place where there were many Outlanders. But in this place there appeared to be no one at all. The antechamber was certainly empty, and so at first I took the hall to be.

The hall itself was impressive enough, with walls that glowed everywhere in a golden diffused light. Indeed the light came equally from the walls, ceiling, and floor, and it was the curious quality of the light which caused me not to notice for a moment a diminutive figure standing there at the far end of the hall. The figure moved, and in the merest fraction of a second I both saw it and recognised it. The heavy gait, balancing carefully in a force field markedly different from terrestrial gravity, could belong to only one person. It was Edelstam.

"Where is everybody?" I asked immediately.

Edelstam gave me a look, partly sly and partly in sorrow. "There's nobody here, except myself. And you, of course, now that you've arrived," he replied.

"You expected me?"

"It was expected, yes. In fact, I've been waiting for you."

"For what?"

In answer, Edelstam took me back to the antechamber, and then to a sliding door that was opened by a switch in the antechamber. Immediately I saw the pack I had carried across the frontier from Russia into Turkey. It was simply sitting there on the floor of a small, entirely closed room. Since by now I had developed a suspicious frame of mind, I immediately walked to the pack, to check its contents. They were substantially the same as they had been when the battery thing had been in my care.

"So you got it through," I admitted, half grudgingly.

"And you got safely through yourself. Congratulations."

Edelstam led me back to the hall, after carefully shutting the sliding door.

"It was not made easy for me. Especially by my friends," I managed to interpose.

"Perhaps not in the beginning. But everything was made easy in the later stages—at least that is my understanding," Edelstam said thoughtfully.

"How do you understand?"

"Peter, we have other things to consider. So let's not waste time with such questions."

I allowed myself to be diverted for the moment, for truth to tell I was unnerved by this place, particularly by the absence of people.

"What other things?" I asked meekly.

"Oh, mainly that responsibility for the pack rests now with you. I've done my part."

"Responsibility for doing what?"

"I can't say."

"Can't say, or you won't say?"

"Can't. I don't know. No doubt you'll be receiving instructions."

"No doubt," I muttered.

"I'll be glad to be getting back. Being alone in this station hasn't been good."

"Getting back!" I exclaimed.

"Of course. I'm returning in Macro's ship. I desperately wanted to come out here for a while, but now I've seen it I won't be sorry to be on my way back to Earth."

"There must be quite a bit that you can tell me."

"Such as what?"

"Well, mundane things. Like exactly where we are.

Where does this force field come from?"

In response to this request, Edelstam gave me a complete tour. He showed me where there were rooms with beds, food, and washing accommodations. Compared to the restricted quarters on Macro's ship, the space around me seemed enormous. But there was one overwhelming disadvantage to it. The station, as Edelstam called it, had no outlets, except through the system of the air locks, of which there seemed to be more than one method of exiting. But to where? Merely into space, somewhere near Jupiter. There was no scanner screen, as there had been in the ship, and it was this lack of a window on the world outside which made the place seem so daunting. I could readily understand Edelstam's wish to be away from it.

"As regards the force field, I don't know," said Edelstam at the end of our tour. "It can't be due to rotation, the way it is in the ships."

"How d'you know that?"

Edelstam laughed at my naïvety. "If we were spinning around, once every few minutes, how could Macro's ship have been docked the way it was? No, it's something much more subtle than that, something more like the operation of the battery device."

Remembering the great power of the battery was curiously comforting. It was an oasis of the remarkable in an otherwise drab desert.

"But where *is* the territory of the Outlanders?" I suddenly asked in desperation.

"Here. You're in it. It's all around you."

"But this isn't *territory.*"

"It's the most you'll ever find."

"But it just isn't possible. I mean for the Outlanders to

144

be supplying the power beams to the Earth. Out of nothing at all."

I knew that I was now coming close to the monstrous things which I had dreaded for so long. Edelstam wedged himself solidly into one of the chairs.

"I can tell you a bit. In fact quite a bit. More, possibly, than you will care to know," he said, reflecting my own thoughts. "It might all seem incredible and incomprehensible to you. Yet it is not so," he went on. "The essence of the matter is that the Outlanders are not responsible for the power beams."

"For God's sake, Edelstam, somebody is responsible for those beams. I've seen them. They're real."

Edelstam chuckled in the back of his throat. "Of course they're real, and of course somebody is responsible for them. But not the Outlanders, not in any basic way. The Outlanders are engineers of a sort. They construct from plans."

"Everybody constructs from plans. So what's remarkable about that?"

"What is remarkable is the origin of the plans."

"How is that?"

Edelstam eased himself in his chair.

"I've made quite a few discoveries in my life," he asserted. "Easily the most remarkable was the thing I'm telling you now. There are wholly different creatures, creatures whom I call the *incandescent ones*. It is these incandescent ones, not the Outlanders, who are responsible for the power beams, and for the battery thing, and for a great deal else besides."

"Where are these incandescent ones?" I asked in as sceptical a tone as I could manage.

"Here, in the vicinity of Jupiter. This is the territory of the incandescent ones, not of the Outlanders."

"But the Outlanders must come from somewhere!" I exclaimed in some desperation now, for Edelstam's peculiar revelation stirred a dark chord within me.

"Doubtless," was the dry response from the little man.

"And I don't see how the Outlanders could work from plans, unless they were in contact with those who supplied the plans."

"The Outlanders are in contact, but not in the way you imagine."

"In what way then?"

"Through ideas in the mind. Ideas appear which seem spontaneous, but which are not really so. The ideas *are* the contact."

Edelstam uncrossed his legs, and then recrossed them in a reversed configuration.

"You mean," I said slowly, "that ideas appear mysteriously, telling us what to do next?"

"Exactly. Telling you what to do next. That's the contact."

"But this would be very difficult to do," I went on, still reaching for my thoughts.

"Not difficult for the incandescent ones. They are not just people, not just very clever people. They are something quite different."

"I don't follow you, Mr. Edelstam."

"Imagine the evolutionary difference between an insect and a human. Imagine a similar difference between the human species and the incandescent ones. Imagine a vast difference of perception of the world. Then you will have the beginning of the right idea."

Edelstam drew in a deep breath, which he then let go

in a long sigh. "It isn't easy to live with such a thought. To know how very small and insignificant you are," he added.

"When did these incandescent ones arrive here?" I asked.

"I think a very long time ago."

"How is it they've never been seen? From the Earth?"

"Does an ant easily see a human?"

"You said these creatures have been here for a very long time. For thousands of years?"

"Much longer than that I think. Perhaps for many millions of years."

"Then they've been here all the time?"

"All the time?"

"All the time Earthlanders have been developing. Through history, and even before that," I explained.

"Yes, that has been so."

I fell silent for a while. Edelstam continued to sit in his chair, his legs stretched out, and his eyes lifted to the luminous ceiling above our heads. So there was nothing out beyond this place, at any rate nothing with a meaning for me. I had come to the confines of what was possible. Yet the pack remained for me to dispose of, unless it was intended that I should remain here indefinitely as its guardian, indefinitely condemned to inhabit the threshold to the world of the incandescent ones.

"Why do you call them incandescent ones?"

"Because they seem to exist in a luminous form."

"So they can be seen?"

"I believe so, for a fleeting moment. I believe I have seen them myself, although I wouldn't dare to say so back on Earth, at an Academy meeting."

Edelstam's remark came as a surprise.

"What is that to an Outlander?" I asked in bewilderment. Edelstam immediately jumped up from the chair, lifting a finger to emphasise his reply, "You don't understand, Peter. I'm not an Outlander. I'm *human.*"

"But why then are you so involved?" I managed to stammer.

"Why shouldn't I be involved?"

"I'd hardly have thought the other Outlanders would go for that." Even as I made this remark I remembered my father's last injunction, never to entrust the battery thing into the keeping of a human. But my father had also told me I would know the man who came to meet me. And I'd known Edelstam and I'd committed the battery thing to his keeping without any emotional qualm. And confirming my judgement, Edelstam had brought it safely through from Earth.

"So you're human, Mr. Edelstam. So maybe that explains the Turkish workmen who were laying for me?" I pointed to my left eye and cheek.

Edelstam lifted his arms and shook his head emphatically. "That part of the plan had absolutely nothing to do with me."

"You gave me the pack with the landmine in it, don't forget," I said angrily, standing threateningly above the little man. Edelstam went on shaking his head, but now in a more sorrowful way.

"Peter, I wanted to avoid having to tell you this. Don't you understand what it is you are?"

"What *I* am?"

"Yes, what all the Outlanders are. You are *robots,* the whole lot of you! When I said before you were engineers, that was a polite way of saying it, don't you see?"

"No, I don't." But I did. In a brief moment I saw a great deal. I saw the dark truth which had lain so long within me, the dark truth which I had so much feared to learn. Then the absurdity struck me, of this little fellow with his own mechanical clockwork gait referring to *me* as a robot, and I barked out at him in the same strange laugh that I'd first used when we met the day at the mountain hut.

Then Edelstam went on to put words to my thoughts. "For the most part," he began, "Outlanders are specialists, designed for a particular function. They manage that particular function superbly well, better than a human would do."

"Designed by whom? The incandescent ones?"

"Obviously."

"I don't feel I have a special function, not particularly."

Edelstam thought for a moment. "I was going to say you're a bit of a specialist on skis, which is true enough. But I think you're something else besides. Unlike the others, who have been programmed always to know what they must do, you're more complex, more all purpose, more given to responding to events as they arise."

While I could see a lot in this, it left much unexplained. "I don't see where my father, and my family, come into that kind of picture."

"Your father?"

"Yes, my father."

"Don't you understand your relation to your father?"

"What relation?"

"Well, I'd have thought it was obvious. But I suppose I'd better tell you, even if you find the idea painful. Your father, as you describe him, was simply the robot you were programmed to take instructions from. Did you ever question what he told you to do?"

"In the mountains I would certainly have questioned his judgement."

"Ah, because you were the specialist there, and *he* was the one programmed to take instructions from you, on that one thing. But otherwise?"

"I suppose I didn't." And in truth I'd always accepted my father's instructions more placidly, more unquestioningly, than would a young human of my own age.

"Did other Outlanders ever give you instructions in a similar way?" Edelstam asked.

"No, they didn't."

"You understand why not?"

"No."

"Because they were programmed to recognise you as being of a superior type. They would play their part in any determined pattern, but they would never presume to offer you advice in a fluid situation."

"Except for my father, I was never able to get much in the way of information out of anybody else."

"Of course not, and if you ever sought gratuitous information from any other Outlander I'll bet they were highly embarrassed by your questions." Edelstam nodded.

Which was true. "You mean that in a kind of way I was the boss?" I asked in surprise.

"I think so." Edelstam continued to nod.

The dark thoughts lightened for a brief moment.

"I still don't understand the business of the Turkish workmen," I repeated, pointing again to my eye.

Edelstam thought a long time before he replied. When he did so his voice was surprisingly low-pitched and gentle. "Peter, it is the nature of a robot to be expendable. When your father could not cross the pass, he was expendable. With your load safely delivered across the pass, *you* were expendable."

"But why?"

"With you gone, there would have been no loose end, no way to discover its continued existence, except through those of us who were concerned to bring it here."

"But why were you involved?"

"With you or with the battery?"

"Both."

"I was involved with you only because the others were strangely squeamish about it. Dolfuss should have been there to meet you at the mountain hut. Because he was so unhappy about it, I had to do it."

"Why did you do it?"

"For the plain *human* reason that it made my position safer. Remember the plan wasn't mine. It was an Outlander plan."

"I can't see your motives, Mr. Edelstam."

"In helping with the battery?"

"Right."

"Well, not every human bothers himself with power and politics. My motive has always been to *learn*. If I hadn't learned many things I wouldn't be able to stand talking to you now, would I?"

"So you learned about the battery?"

"And about many other things besides. Because I was trusted. You see, Peter, the real concern of the incandescent ones is with humans, not with the Outlanders. The Outlanders are only a means to that end. So there has never been any objection to *me* learning, so long as my motives were pure, as you might say."

I pointed to my eye, to remind him again of the Turkish workmen.

"Was this very pure?" I asked.

"It was not my plan," he answered blandly. "If it had been my plan I would have felt differently about it."

"Can I ask a different kind of question, Mr. Edelstam?"

"Why not?"

"I'd like to know in what way the two of us are really different. You speak of me as a robot, of me being programmed to do certain things. O.K. Suppose I accept that. But what of you? Aren't you just a robot in your own way, programmed just as certainly to do your own thing?"

Edelstam thought about this for what seemed a very long time. I suppose I might say there was a cloudy, puzzled look on his face. At length he gave a wry grin.

"I'm not going to take my stand on a question of the soul," he said, "although there are a lot of people of my faith who would do just that. Maybe I *am* programmed. But I am programmed through the relation of mankind to the whole world."

"And I'm programmed by the incandescent ones?"

"Right."

"But maybe it's better to be programmed by a creature who knows exactly what it's doing than by a blind relationship to the whole world. Mr. Edelstam, on reflection I'm prepared to assert that you, as a human, are nothing but a random creature, a freak of fate, whereas I and my kind are of a purposive construction, well designed by a great and subtle intellect."

I spoke half in jest, but Edelstam I could see was deeply worried by my unexpected line of argument. He kept on searching for a way to justify his position, to justify the dignity of the human species, I suppose.

"It would depend on the depth of purpose," he admitted at last.

"Do we know that?"

"I can't say for you, Peter. But for some of the Outlanders the purpose cannot be particularly deep."

"Is it deep for all humans?"

This silenced him again. Not wishing to bring the discussion to a dead stop, I went on, "Give me one or two examples."

"Well, can I take your own father?"

"O.K." I nodded, although I felt sensitive about it.

"Do you understand the nature of your father's speciality?"

"Not very well. But I think it was in what humans would call 'counterintelligence.' "

"No, no, not at all. His intelligence activities were scarcely more than a matter of straightforward programming. His real speciality was quite a bit more remarkable than that, but with clear-cut limitations nonetheless."

"How was that?"

"Well, Peter, exactly how did your father work the battery?"

"I don't know."

"Did you try to work it yourself?"

"I had a look at it. But I could see no means of working it. There seemed to be no controls."

"There are none on the outside certainly."

"But how could he get at the inside?" I asked.

"That's precisely the point. Your father had special radiative circuits, inside the head I would imagine, that communicated into the interior of the battery. You don't have those circuits. I don't have them. I can't work the battery any more than you can, although I'm supposed to be an expert in experimental physics. So your father's speciality was very peculiar, very particular, very remarkable, but it was a strictly limited function. It was exactly the kind of function to be expected from a cleverly designed robot."

Although I couldn't understand the logic whereby my father thus became inferior to humans who couldn't do anything remarkable at all, I felt oddly enough that Edelstam had scored a point. The feeling led me to persist with a recollection I would otherwise never have allowed to come out in words.

"You know," I said, "just before his own death, my father said that it was necessary for him to keep faith with the dead. I've often wondered what he meant by it."

It took Edelstam scarcely ten seconds to come out with an answer.

"The battery isn't only a source of raw power. It has the ability to direct power in very particular ways. I think you must have seen that for yourself?"

I nodded, and Edelstam went on, "To do that there must be ordered information within it, as well as an energy source. In short, it must contain a data bank. My guess would be that the dead are stored in that data bank."

"The dead!" I exclaimed in real astonishment.

"By the dead I mean the memory circuits of the dead, and I think that's what your father must also have meant. Quite likely his own memory circuit is stored there now."

"You mean they could all be restored?"

"Yes, it would be in the nature of a robot that it could be restored."

I knew I now had the vital information from Edelstam towards which I'd been subconsciously working. So with the feeling, wrong as it turned out, that I would learn nothing further of much significance from him, I made no objection when shortly afterwards he indicated a desire to take his leave. While he went off to pack a few things, I was left contemplating the situation. So this was it. I was

154

now the lone custodian of the dead. Like my father I would also keep faith with them.

The picture was nearly complete, but there were still a few details which didn't quite fit or which I didn't understand. There was Macro making a huge circle with his arm. Even very minor matters like that must take their place in the pattern. It was hard to credit that Sam Ossett's infallible memory for the fall of cards was also a part of it. Yet there was a clue in Sam's play to the implacable accuracy of the whole affair.

A plan may contain conditional elements: If X happens, follow design A; if Y happens, follow design B. Something of this kind must, I saw, be applicable to the incident of the Turkish workmen. If I'd failed to survive the incident, then, as Edelstam had pointed out, no investigation through me could have led to a knowledge of the continuing existence of the battery. But because I had actually survived, a different plan had come into operation, one in which I had now become the custodian of the battery, as my father had been before me. I saw that it was the conditional nature of the plan which had caused difficulty for Dolfuss, and for the other Outlanders. The new design, I suspected, had still to reach its climax.

It was not long before Edelstam reappeared, his packing done. He looked more cheerful and spritely than I'd seen him before.

"I guess Mary and the grandchildren will be glad to see me back," he said.

"You'll be wanting to be on your way."

"Sure. Sure. Now, Peter, don't start fretting about things. Try to forget that little conversation of ours."

"Just a word of advice before you go, Mr. Edelstam."

"Always glad of a bit of advice."

"Watch out you don't start playing cards with a fellow called Sam Ossett. At least, if you do, don't play with real money."

As Edelstam turned to make his way to the connecting bridge which led to Macro's ship, I suppressed the impulse to speak to him about human death. It was on the tip of my tongue to tell him that as the moment approached for his own death he should try to console himself with the thought that he too was only a robot, and therefore expendable in the great scheme of things. But I sensed that he was less able to take such a prospect than I was. So at the last moment, in pity, I desisted.

It was then that the light behind us suddenly brightened.

"What goes on?" muttered Edelstam.

He moved ahead of me, once again with his pounding gait, back to the hall we had just quitted. I heard him shout, "Jeez!" just before I saw it myself. One of the walls, with its soft diffused light, had been replaced by the brilliantly coloured surface of the planet Jupiter, as if the wall itself had become a viewing screen. The magnificence of the sight was totally without parallel in my experience. We weren't looking from a distance. We were right up against the thing.

"Are we looking out now?" I asked.

Edelstam shook his head. "No," he answered, "not directly. This is being done electronically. It's a projection on a kind of super screen. But my guess is that from outside this station it really does look like that."

"As big as that?"

"I guess so."

"A bit spooky, isn't it?"

"Sure is. I'll be glad to be on my way." So saying, Edelstam gave a shudder. "Not a nice place to be," he concluded. I pointed towards two bright columns which reared up until they were lost at the edge of the screen.

"Fuel, I would think. I'm betting those columns are heated by laser beams directed downwards into Jupiter."

"What kind of fuel?"

"Deuterium. The stuff used in nuclear fusion. It's very high grade—if you know how to use it. Better than the ordinary hydrogen which the Sun uses."

"Isn't there any on the Earth? Is that the trouble with human power resources?"

"No, not at all. There's plenty of deuterium on the Earth, everywhere in ordinary water. The trouble isn't the lack of fuel. The trouble is volume."

"Volume?" I asked in surprise.

"The stuff has to be heated in a real big space, the way it's done here in the atmosphere of Jupiter. That's how the power beams to the Earth are generated."

Edelstam took me firmly by the arm. Pointing toward Jupiter with its many colours, ochres, browns, and purples, he went on, "You know, there's enough energy down there to keep the Earth going for longer even than the age of the whole universe."

"If you knew how to use it."

"Right, if we knew, the way the incandescent ones know. That's why learning is so important, more important than power and politics."

With a sense of shock we both recoiled a few steps from the glowing wall, for suddenly the image there disappeared. Then a heavily muffled figure appeared high up on the right.

"It's monstrous," I shouted, "absolutely monstrous!"

The figure appeared to be on skis, skis which sparkled like a firework display. It twisted and turned, spiralling downward like a man in a slalom race. Then it was gone, and the bright edge of Jupiter came back on the screen.

Edelstam gave his deep, throaty chuckle, but I could see no humour in the situation.

"Well," he burbled, "that's got to mean something. Skiing it is. But where? Not on White Mountain. Skiing close to Jupiter. You'd need a space suit for that."

It was then that the potential significance of the space suit, with which Macro had equipped me, burst upon my mind. When I told Edelstam about it he laughed still more openly.

"Sure looks as though this is it. Instead of mouldering here, you're intended to go somewhere, somewhere over Jupiter. But I don't get this business of circling." Edelstam waved his arm, the way Macro and the crewmen had done.

The figure appeared again on the screen, this time on the lower left. Flames burst from the skis, and in a flash the figure appeared to soar upward, disappearing at the very top of the screen.

"Whew," I whistled between my teeth. "I've never seen anything like that before. Was he really going up?"

"Looked like it. Surely did. So maybe we'd better try to argue it out."

"I don't see how you can argue a thing like that."

Edelstam scratched his head and then pointed upwards with a finger. "If you asked me if it was possible to ski in the atmosphere of Jupiter, I'd say no." At this, I simply grunted. "But if you were to tell me I'm wrong," Edelstam went on, "I'd want to know where the support

158

would come from, support against the downward pull of gravity."

"That's obvious, even to me," I growled.

Undeterred, Edelstam continued, "Maybe by magnetic forces. Jupiter has a strong magnetic field—for a planet. But you'd need a big flow of electric current, too big to be possible, I'd say."

"A big flow where?"

"In your skis, of course."

"But something *was* happening in the skis," I said, with the beginnings of interest in Edelstam's argument.

"Sure, something was happening. A lot was happening. So maybe I'm not being so crazy after all?"

The figure now appeared for the third time on the screen, dark and heavily muffled as it always seemed to be. This time the motion was quite uncontrolled. The lone skier was falling head over heels, falling downwards towards Jupiter.

"That guy is through," shouted Edelstam. But he was wrong. With a brilliant flash from the skis, the tumbling motion stopped and the figure glided smoothly away to the left.

"Jack and Jill went up the hill . . ." Edelstam said, chuckling.

"How d'you sort that one out?"

"I've got ideas. Oh, how I've got ideas."

"I'd like to hear them."

"Well, it's the battery thing all over again, isn't it?"

"Could be. Something pretty powerful seems to be involved."

"I reckon I told you before why I call it a battery," Edelstam reminded me.

"Something to do with an electromotive force, wasn't it?"

"Right. An EMF. It produces an electric current when it operates in a conductor. Which is what it might do in the metal of those skis the fellow was wearing. O.K.?"

"I reckon so. It figures," I agreed. Edelstam was becoming excited now. He took me confidentially by the elbow. "Look, young fellow, imagine yourself to be wearing skis equipped with a battery."

"One battery or two?"

"Why would it matter?" Edelstam asked. I saw no point in explaining, so I indicated that he should continue.

"You want to generate a large electric current running the length along your skis."

"Why do I want to do that?"

"Because by directing the current the right way you can make Jupiter's magnetic field push upward on the skis, like the ground pressing upward when you ski in a normal way. It would be great if you could do that."

"Great?"

"Well, by making the current a bit too weak for full support you'd tend to fall down. As you fell you'd pick up speed. O.K.?"

"O.K."

"Then by strengthening the current you'd overcompensate for gravity, and then . . ."

"Then you'd soar," I interrupted.

"Right! Just like that guy was doing. But there's still one big trouble. Where does all this current go to? You can't have the current going one way in one ski and the opposite way in the other ski."

Here Edelstam's chuckle rumbled out once more.

"Then you'd have a push up on one ski and a pull down

on the other. You'd sure go arse over tip." Striding up and down, he went on in the manner of a lecturer, "No, the current has to go the same way in both skis. So what happens at the ends of the skis? Well, at one end a current must go out, and at the other end it must come in. The current must be continuous. Kirchoff's law." Even though this was becoming a bit technical, I let him go on. "The problem before us," proclaimed Edelstam in an oratorical style, "is the manner of flow of the current *outside* the skis." He emphasised the word 'outside' with a raised finger. "The big question now is this: What material is it that bears the current outside? A gas discharge of some kind. O.K.? Am I making myself clear?"

"Sort of, I guess."

"Now I doubt there could be sufficient gas in the normal atmosphere of Jupiter. The atmosphere is too thin. So you'd have to carry a supply with you, along with your life support system."

"A supply of gas?" This was a surprise, for Macro had made no mention of a supply of gas.

"Right! Now you couldn't be supplying gas all the time. You couldn't carry enough. So the gas would have to move along with you. You'd create a kind of cloud around you."

"A cloud of gas?" I repeated woodenly, like a stage character.

"Yeah, and all the time there'd be an enormous current through the gas. Which would do what?"

"What?"

"It would heat the gas. Make it glow. Like a big fire-cracker. Which was just what we saw on the screen right now, wasn't it?"

"How about the one who seemed to be falling?"

"That's more difficult. Suppose we come to it later."

"What would happen if you didn't have any of this gas?"

"It wouldn't work. Nothing would happen."

"When you switched on the batteries?"

"Right. The system would be dead."

"So you'd fall."

"You surely would."

"What sort of gas would it be?"

"Hydrogen might be best. Most electrons for a given weight. But maybe it would be too bulky. Maybe ordinary water. Except it might freeze. This isn't a severe problem. Forget it."

"You seem to have it all worked out, Mr. Edelstam. In theory. The trouble is I may have to do it in practice."

Edelstam held up his finger again. "Worked out? What happens to the forces on the gas? Why doesn't the gas blow itself apart? How can it ride along? Tell me that!"

"I'm listening, Professor."

"There's just one way it might happen. If the flow of the current outside the skis were of the form physicists call 'force-free,' the thing might work. Which means the current must flow parallel to the magnetic field. The problem then is to close the current loop, and that's what I can't quite figure out."

Edelstam resumed his pacing back and forth. "Unless," he said, again with a raised finger, "unless this is a matter of operator skill."

"How could that be?"

"Maybe that's the essential part of this game, to keep the gas moving along with you. On a mountain back on Earth, the skill lies in riding out the bumps in the ground. Here I think the skill will lie in holding the gas along with you. There won't be anything like the same sort of choppy ride. It will be smoother."

162

"It didn't look all that smooth. Not when that fellow was turning head over heels," I objected.

"I said we'd come to that problem later. Well, I'll come to it now. There are all manner of rising columns coming up out of Jupiter. Some are probably natural, connected with variations of the hydrogen-helium mixture deep inside the planet. Others are artificially generated by the laser beams. You can think of these places rather like the rapids in an otherwise fairly placid stream."

"You think the guy went down through one of them?"

"Likely enough. At these places, maybe there's no possibility for keeping the current flow going. So what happens? You simply fall, helter-skelter. And you've got to fall to the other side of these places, otherwise you'd keep on going, right down into Jupiter itself."

"I think *you* should be making this trip."

"Oh, no! This is a young man's sport," came the answer with a chuckle. "Think of these bad places as a kind of whirlpool. If you hit one of 'em, you'll lose all the gas you're carrying with you. Certain to do. So you'll need to resupply the gas somehow. The idea will be to judge the right moment. My guess is the guy we were watching right now was doing exactly that."

"How fast would he be going?"

Edelstam threw back his head and thought for a while. Then, shaking his head, he replied, "Damn fast. Faster than anything you've ever seen. How fast is a ski race? Maybe a hundred miles an hour, at most. Forty metres to a second. I reckon you could go more than a hundred times faster than that. By falling in the field of Jupiter. In fact you could go a lot faster still. Allow yourself to fall along a gentle curve, at a downward angle of a few degrees, as if you were on a slightly inclined snowfield. O.K.?"

"It sounds impossibly fast."

"Not necessarily. Just remember this, compared to anything you're used to, it's all pretty smooth."

"When that guy was falling it didn't look too smooth at all," I insisted.

"He wasn't hitting the ground, remember. He was falling through space."

"O.K. He was falling through space."

"Well, to continue. Suppose you've made it down a gentle curve. What d'you do now?"

"What do I do?" I echoed.

"You soar, my boy," he answered. "Up you go, and then down another gentle curve. Then soar again. Every time down you pick up speed. Without losing it when you soar. O.K.?"

"Sounds great."

"By golly, you could really pick up some speed."

"How would I check the speed?"

"Don't spoil the picture. I was just getting enthusiastic. How do you check speed? Let's work it out. Suppose the magnetic field goes across from left to right, call it north to south. To get support against gravity you must point your skis east to west. Suppose you're racing along at fifty kilometres a second. How do you check speed? Ah-ha, obvious, isn't it?"

"Not to me it isn't."

"Just lie back at an angle of forty-five degrees. In fact, if you want to increase speed, lean forward. If you want to check speed, lean back. Easy."

"But how am I to know which way the field goes?"

"There you go again. Just as soon as I get enthusiastic."

The lone skier appeared on the great screen yet again. This time he wove a complex path, in and out, up and down. Mysterious flashes appeared ahead of him from time to time. Surprisingly, he disappeared from the screen at much the same place as he'd come on to it.

"That manoeuvrability was better than I'd expected. It all seems to work splendidly," Edelstam stated in real surprise.

"What were those flashes?"

"I'm trying to work that one out. I think the guy must have been carrying a gun."

"A gun! What for?"

"For examining the magnetic field."

The gun Macro had given me, which made only a fizzing sound, came instantly to my mind.

"How would a gun be of use for that?" I asked, without explaining to Edelstam.

"Suppose the bullets exploded and scattered some material which followed the contours of the field—say like iron filings around a magnet. Then you would know what lay ahead of you. Great, great!"

"You might know if there was a whirlpool?"

"Absolutely right. It's a great idea."

"How long would it take?" I asked, seeking for the last bits of information.

"How long?"

"Yes, to make a circuit of Jupiter."

"Well, at fifty kilometres to each second you'd get completely around Jupiter in a few hours. A life support system should last much longer than that. Here! An easy way to judge time is by the rotation of Jupiter. The planet goes once round in about ten hours. So if you keep pace with the rotation you know you'll be round in ten hours. If you

165

go ahead of Jupiter you'll be around sooner. If you lag behind, you'll be around slower."

"I get it. But how do I know how *far* I'm round?"

"Watch the stars, I guess."

The picture on the wall disappeared as instantaneously as it had appeared. In spite of the gentle radiance, the hall around us seemed suddenly drab. Within me there was a matching drabness, from which I knew my racy Earth-style conversation with Edelstam had reached the limit of its usefulness. But when I indicated that it was time for him to be on his way, he looked up at me and said,

"Sure you won't be needing me around?"

"I'm sure Macro won't be enjoying having to wait this long."

"I guess not." Edelstam sighed. I picked up his bag in sadness, feeling strangely sorry for this little human, who had just helped me so much.

I saw him to the first of the air locks, where he put on a space suit which he had stored in a room nearby. He waved as he stepped into the lock, and I waved in reply. I knew he was the last I would ever see of his kind.

I had wanted Edelstam to be on his way for two reasons. I wanted to make my preparations in my own good time, not hurriedly, as I would have had to do if he had stayed around. And I wanted to be free from interruptions to my own inner thoughts. Fine as Edelstam's scientific arguments had been, I knew that I would react instinctively when the time came for me to leave. I had reached the end of a long road, a journey cluttered by people and by circumstances not of my own choosing. Now, at last, I was going home. A human might have called it faith, but to me my belief was something more than faith.

But first there were a lot of simple, rational things to do. First, I had to find the skis. I found them in another hall, a smaller one, but with the same suffused light, which I reached by the alternate route through the air locks, the route I'd noted at an earlier stage. I assembled my space suit and the pack with the battery there beside the skis. They were mounted in a booth which stood in the middle of the hall. Also in the booth was a second pack with connections that could be made to the space suit. Since I could not carry two packs, the discovery of the second pack told me what I already suspected, that the battery in my own pack was to be used to power the skis. There was exactly the same iridescence about it when I took it out, the same curious shape. The shape I found to be precisely what was needed for it to be fitted into one of the skis. These I must explain were much bigger than the slender variety I was accustomed to. They were long like ordinary skis, but broad like showshoes. No quick ma- noeuvre would be possible with them, because the whole of the leg had to be fitted into a chain-metal housing.

One of the skis had a battery already, so I used mine to power the other ski. I'd little doubt that the two batteries had both come from Earth—they were the two my father had told me about during our journey through the upland snows of Georgia so long ago.

Once I was standing within the housings of the skis, I put on the upper part of my space suit, to the front of which I clipped a small panel, on which were mounted a number of control buttons. I would have liked to know their function, but I saw no way to discover this informa- tion except by getting started, and by trying them one by one when I was actually in motion. The second pack clipped neatly on to the back of the space suit. This I guessed was the container for the supply of gas which I would need, should I encounter 'whirlpools' in the magnetic field of Jupiter. It was clear already that I would have to be exceedingly careful about the use of this gas, since the supply of it was obviously limited. I thought carefully about this point as I connected the fittings from the pack to the control panel. The last step was to close my space helmet and then to test the life support system according to the procedure Macro and his crew had taught me.

By now I understood that I would not be skiing at all in the usual free sense. All the accoutrements produced a kind of hybrid between skiing and driving a bob sleigh. Less delicate balancing and more driving than free skiing.

I went through the process of assembly three times, to make sure I had everything right, before I permitted myself to touch the control buttons. The first two I pressed did nothing. But at the third there was a brilliant flash, and I found myself gliding clear of the booth.

I thought for a second that I would crash immediately into the wall towards which I was heading. But the control button had also activated an opening in the wall. Rather like a ski jumper coming to the end of his preliminary run, I shot out through the opening into space. A distant Sun, some twenty-five times less brilliant then the Sun I had seen so often from Earth, lay on my left. The planet Jupiter lay below, toward the right. I was on my way.

Flames spurted from my feet. This would be 'corona' caused by the enormous current which was now emerging from each of my skis. Deliberately I asked myself: Were the skis equally balanced? Yes, I decided, unaware of exactly how I reached the decision. Indeed the skis were almost uncomfortably sensationless, until I lifted the tips cautiously. Then I could feel a braking resistance. Moving the tips downwards, I had the sensation of an instantly steepening gradient, as if one could adjust at will the slope of the mountainside down which one was skiing. I was surprised at the lightness of it all.

The corona from my feet spread itself out into a curiously twisted pattern. It began by turning sharply at right angles to the direction of my motion, maintaining a system of smaller helices, inset, it seemed, into larger helices. I found the details of this pattern changed whenever I moved either or both of my skis, but always there remained the system of glowing helices. This would be the gas cloud which I was carrying along with me. I found there was a button for replenishing it, should the gas become peeled away in some untoward incident.

I had fixed Macro's gun to my right gauntlet. I tried firing it. Instead of the seemingly useless fizz it had made before, a new pattern appeared well ahead, a pattern quite different from the twisted blue-violet helices of the gas clouds that swept along with me. This new pattern was in red and it had curtains which reminded me of a terrestrial aurora. The curtains were directed, on this first occasion, in quite straight lines, in a direction at right angles to my motion. This was the direction of the magnetic field in which I was now riding.

I also checked the watch that Macro had given me. It was beginning to turn from the zero position, the first motion it had made since I'd been given it. I began to see now what Macro had intended by his arm circling. I had to make the pointer on the watch circle around in a similar way.

I wasn't aware of any gradient. Yet I must have been picking up speed very rapidly. The scene below me was quite splendid. I had skied in a relaxed fashion down many a gentle snowfield. The best time for such a terrestrial experience is usually about an hour before sundown. But nothing in my experience compared with this floating over Jupiter. The planet filled about half of my range of vision. It was truly enormous. In a way it had a warm, bright feel about it. Better, I thought, than the drabness of the place I'd just left, or than Mars. Although the Sun was so much farther away than on Earth, there was no suggestion of gloom. Jupiter was so large, and its clouds reflected such a high proportion of the Sun's light, that, on the contrary, the scene was exceedingly brilliant. The coloured details of Jupiter's surface markings were even more striking from out here than they'd been in the hall where Edelstam and I had held our last discussion.

By about this time I began to suspect that, so far as this skiing business was concerned, the learned Edelstam hadn't told me quite the whole of the story. Either that or I hadn't understood him properly. I was poised now pretty well directly above the equator of the planet. A shot from my gun had told me that the magnetic field was going pretty much like the lines of longitude on a geographical globe. To relate to such a geographical picture, I was headed now along the equator, in a direction from west to east, that is to say in the same direction as Jupiter itself was rotating.

The planet was going faster than I was, a lot faster. But not so much faster as in the beginning. It followed therefore that I was still picking up speed. So far so good. My skis at this time were pointed downhill at about forty-five degrees. Yet the strange thing, the thing I hadn't expected, was that I didn't seem to be falling.

The pressure in my legs was fairly close to terrestrial

gravity, a bit stronger perhaps. This meant that I couldn't be simply hovering like an eagle, with my weight exactly compensated by the magnetic thrust in the skis. I knew this because my weight at the start had been only about two-thirds of terrestrial gravity. So a part of the thrust should be either pushing me upwards or pushing me forwards. I decided it must be pushing me forwards.

I tried varying the controls, especially the control which changed the strength of the current passing through the skis. Increasing the strength increased the thrust in my legs. Gradually I learned the range over which I felt reasonably comfortable. There was a control for ejecting gas from the pack on my back, but I was reluctant to play with this, because it was so obviously important to conserve the supply as much as possible. I experimented with the orientation of the skis. The thrust was stronger when they were directed along the equatorial direction, which was the direction my 'watch' was telling me to go. But I could reduce the thrust to nothing at all, simply by turning at right angles, and so directing my skis towards the pole of Jupiter. In fact, one could operate the skis just by seeking for maximum thrust, keeping the current control fixed for this purpose of course.

However, there was the seemingly strange ambiguity to which I've already referred. However much I tilted the skis downwards towards Jupiter, the thrust stayed always the same. I even tried a kind of nose-dive position, with the skis pointing vertically downwards. The thrust still stayed the same, pushing me wholly forwards in the direction I was supposed to go. I decided that in this position I simply must be falling towards Jupiter, since the thrust was then doing nothing to support my weight. Quickly, I reverted to the forty-five-degree downward angle, which seemed best suited for progress, at any rate according to the needle on the watch that Macro had given to me.

My course was taking me directly toward a dark red spot in the cloud structure of Jupiter. This wasn't the Great Red Spot, although it was something like it, only smaller. I used it as a navigation marker. More precisely, the rotation of Jupiter was carrying the spot towards me, for I wasn't travelling as fast as the planet was spinning, as yet.

No sooner had this spot come directly below than the halo of gas around me was whisked away, and the thrust in my skis instantly disappeared. I was weightless now and therefore presumably falling. Not vertically, because by now I'd acquired quite a considerable sideways motion, which I knew would bring me eventually clear of this dead magnetic area. I decided all I had to do was to fall across the spot area, and then continue as before, using my precious store of gas to create a new cloud. But slowly I began to turn and twist. Neither Jupiter nor the Sun would stay in the places where they were supposed to be. Nothing remained fixed, and in this senseless disorder I began to panic. My fear was that, because I had lost all sense of orientation, I'd never be able to judge the moment when I came clear of the dead area.

Instinctively, I seized on a last resort to judge the situation. I waited for the rare moments when Jupiter appeared straight above me—in other words when my head was pointed downwards. Then I tried to judge whether the red spot was located strictly at the centre of Jupiter's disk. As soon as I felt convinced the spot was definitely off-centre, I decided I must have fallen through the dead area, and therefore it was now appropriate to eject gas and to begin the current drive again. After checking the appropriate control on my tunic I started the gas ejector system, and to my intense relief a small thrust in my legs started at once. Luckily I had proceeded gingerly. Because of my tumbling motion there was no ordered thrust from the skis. Sometimes they would push me to the right, sometimes to the left, sometimes up, sometimes down. If the thrust had been strong I would have had no chance at all of ever bringing the situation under control.

In a curiously instinctive way—how I did it I could not describe—I managed to stop the tumbling motion. Once I'd righted myself, the thrust could be increased, and my course could be reset. All this I did. Everything was fine again. I'd come through my first crisis. Except I'd used up some gas, and I was lower down than I'd been before, definitely closer to Jupiter.

It was only then that I took a look at my 'watch.' To my horror the needle had moved backwards. And since it continued to move backwards, I concluded I was now on a wrong course.

Where was the mistake? Perhaps I should have avoided the spot. Yet the watch had directed me towards it. What I had *not* done was to look at the watch while I was tumbling. With the sickening thought that I should really have used the watch to tell me *when* I should pull out of the fall, I wondered if I'd pulled out too soon, or too late.

There was no point in continuing along a wrong path. I was on a losing game all the time now. With an intense determination I therefore decided deliberately to cut the current, to go back into the tumble, to fall still closer down towards Jupiter.

This time as I lost control of balance I made no attempt to orient myself with respect to Jupiter. I concentrated entirely on the watch. It soon ceased to go backwards. So

I'd been right to decide on a second fall. The watch went slowly forwards as my tumble continued, endlessly on and on, it seemed.

I became quite bemused in this unorganized world of lights and of colours. My only point of control with the normal world of the senses was the instrument on my wrist. In a world of dissolving consciousness I concentrated just on the needle, as it moved by the slightest amount. But now it was moving backwards again. This was the moment I must pull out of my dive.

Correction was harder this time. I'd been falling longer and I was spinning faster. Yet, with the practice I'd had on the first occasion, I found it possible to stop the spinning. Again I used the thrust in the skis, which I'd started up once more, in a wholly instinctive way. I could no more write down what I did than I could write down a description of all the movements of a slalom race. So far as I was concerned, you just did it. Or you didn't do it. In which case you ended up inside Jupiter.

The planet was now terrifyingly close. The atmosphere seemed to form a carpet not far below my feet. To avoid sinking lower the thrust in my legs had to be larger than terrestrial gravity, considerably larger. Since there would be no possibility of my maintaining this situation for very long, it followed I must move upwards. What was the word Edelstam had used? Soar. I must soar. Except that at a thrust approaching 2g, soaring was the last thing I felt like doing.

There was nothing for it but to increase the current drive. The thrust became abominable. What made me take it at all was the thought that I would hardly have been started on an impossible journey. So this soaring just had to be possible. Except that my mistake had probably

174

taken me closer to Jupiter than I need have gone. In an agony of tension I checked that the needle on my watch was still going the right way. I just had to hang on.

As my distance from Jupiter increased, the thrust required to balance my weight became less, and so the thrust required to maintain an additional soaring motion naturally also became less. As the tension eased, my legs developed a violent spasm of trembling.

So far I'd been content simply to rise. Now that the tension was less, it became possible to develop a further sideways motion. Once again I took a stance leaning forwards with my skis at a forty-five-degree angle and with the current drive just about sufficient to support my weight, which at last had become tolerable again. I reckoned the soaring motion had occupied upwards of half an hour. It had been as tough a proposition, from the point of view of strength of leg, as the longest ski run I'd ever done.

The next section of the journey was quite trouble free. I picked up more and more orbital speed around the equator of the planet, which made the thrust needed to support my weight become less and less. This went on until the pointer on the watch indicated that half the journey was completed. Everything seemed set fair. Then I ran over two further dead areas. By now, however, I had sufficient height for the resulting falls to be not too serious. The trouble was that I needed a further discharge of gas after each fall. Nothing worked when you were over these dead zones. You simply had to fall through, hoping you didn't fall too far.

After the second of these further episodes, I was startled to notice a red light on the front of my suit, and an unknown ghostly voice whispering in my headpiece.

"You have left only one further charge of gas." This was bad, real bad, a punishment for my mistake. I had gratuitously wasted gas. This was more important than lost time, or lost distance. From then on, to the end of the journey, I was haunted by the fear of my gas supply becoming exhausted. The next dead area would then lead to disaster.

The trouble was that dead areas could strike you without warning. If you were lucky enough to use the magnetic indicator gun just at the right moment, then perhaps you might detect them ahead. But not very far ahead, not far enough to take much in the way of avoiding action. The best idea seemed to be to keep away from the kind of areas on Jupiter, like the red spots, which indicated their presence. It was a bit the same as a glider pilot on Earth trying to spot those places on the ground which generate updrafts. Hard to do, but perhaps not impossible. If you were experienced enough, which I wasn't.

The magnetic indicator gun showed up something quite new, not too far ahead. The red auroral streaks, instead of being oriented in straight lines, were now disordered, in curves and twists. This disordered structure in the field wasn't a dead spot. A dead spot was a place of no field. Here the problem was a jumble of irregularities, with the red streaks looking like a ball of wool.

The natural thing to do was to cut the current in my skis, so that the rapidly varying thrusts wouldn't tear me apart. The convenient thing would have been to cut the current altogether and then simply to fall through the trouble. But this would lose my accompanying gas cloud, which wasn't even to be thought of. Somehow I'll have to try really skiing through this thing, I thought grimly to myself. Then I was into it. The twists and turns were as devilish as anything I'd ever encountered on a terrestrial mountain. Here the situation was complicated by the astonishing variations of the forces. On Earth, forces are predominantly downwards. Here they could be upwards as well as downwards, and they could go sideways at any angle. There was just one advantage. The forces on the two skis were always equal.

It was a strange business. While the rolls and twists had a greater variety than anything I'd experienced before, they were quite slow and deliberate. There was none of the split-second timing of a difficult terrestrial situation. A mistake on a mountain leads to a fall which may be serious —a broken leg perhaps—but which is never less than painful. Here a mistake would not so much be painful as totally confusing. One would tumble and twist, roll and fall, in a hopeless situation, probably spinning up to a degree which could never be checked.

I made frequent use now of the magnetic indicator, to a point where I began to wonder how long it would continue to fire. It was a bit like surf riding in truly gigantic ocean waves, except that here I found myself gliding up and down the waves with my skis in a sideways position, parallel to the wave crests, not at right angles to them.

I emerged at length at the far side of this tangled magnetic ball of wool. From an infinite distance it seemed, the ghostly voice murmured in my ear. So I was being watched all the time. In a way I had to be, otherwise how could the watch thing on my wrist keep telling me how I was doing? I was glad to find the pointer had crept still further around its circuit, still in the favorable direction.

The disk of Jupiter was steadily getting less. Not dramatically so; it still filled nearly half of my field of vision. But getting less nevertheless, which told me I was rising—soaring again. I found I got the best response from the moving pointer when I levelled off my skis, instead of pointing them downwards. I tried reducing the current flow, but this didn't help. Nor did pointing my skis upwards. Which all went to convince me that I had to stop increasing my orbital speed, but that the time hadn't come yet for slowing down. I still had some way to go.

An exceedingly black round spot on the surface of Jupiter swept below me. I watched it with the sickening thought that the last of my gas supply would now be gone. Then with a profound sense of relief I realised this was only a shadow, a shadow cast by one of Jupiter's satellites. Which? I couldn't find it. Then I realised it must be directly above my head, and directly above my head there was the glare of the Sun. It occurred to me how lucky I'd been not to have to tackle the magnetic ball of wool with the Sun shining directly in my face.

The soaring continued, until I became convinced my speed had now become so great that I would be projected away into space. Yet I wasn't going around much faster than Jupiter was spinning. Did this mean I was still attached to the planet? I couldn't decide. So I remained satisfied by the pointer on the watch, which showed me to be still reasonably on course.

A strange brilliance appeared above the limb of Jupiter, in the direction of my motion. Without looking directly towards it, at first I took it to be the Sun. But only a short time ago the Sun had been above my head, so it couldn't be the Sun. Nor was the thing as intense as the disk of the Sun. It was, however, a good deal more intense than the disk of Jupiter. It was much smaller than Jupiter, more like a satellite. Yet no satellite could be as bright as this.

I guessed this brightly radiant region might be the main nuclear power generator, which I hoped might mean that my destination was not far away. Unfortunately, however, the pointer on my watch showed that more than a quarter of the journey still lay ahead. Besides I hadn't begun to check speed at all yet.

The optimum path indicated by the needle took me directly towards the thing. It was also taking me ever higher and higher above Jupiter. Because a general brilliance of light now suffused the sky—the thing was so close —it wasn't possible any longer to use the magnetic gun. I hit another magnetic ball of wool without warning. As I've said already, it was like trying to ride a series of enormous ocean waves. On the previous occasion I'd had some idea of where I was going, thanks to the gun. Now I had no idea. The suffused brilliance all around me was totally confusing.

I lost control. Unfortunately I took one of the waves with my skis slanted at a wrong angle, overturned, and then was unable to recover. It is true there was no hard slope to fall on. But forces snatched at me, buffeting me in seemingly random directions. With the horrifying thought that my skis might be totally wrenched away, I cut the current once again. Instantly the hammering ceased. I continued to twist but not too quickly and without too much unpleasant sensation, except when I opened my eyes I found the world to be a meaningless smear of bright colour.

I took my disoriented condition for as long as I felt I could. Then I eased open the gas jet, ever so slightly. Anxiously I tried to convince myself of an answering pressure in my legs. But there was none, so I had to continue tumbling and pitching. This unrestrained motion was so

179

slow and deliberate, the swings had become so large, that sickness appeared inevitable, the most ghastly seasickness. Knowing this would be a total disaster, spewing all through the interior of my suit, I steeled myself to stop any convulsive ejection of my stomach. The pitching and rolling continued without a moment's respite.

At length I tried a second spurt of gas, but only later, after a third attempt, following still another appalling episode, did I obtain some pressure in my skis. Cautiously I increased the gas flow, feeling that my last reserves were now being used. The tension in my legs built up more and more, to a degree where I could once again seek gradually to check the spinning motion.

Dizzy, sick, and exhausted, I came at last to a controlled position. The bright radiance which had so nearly spelled disaster lay now behind me. I found just enough determination to regret that I'd not been able to get a close look at it.

I tried uptilting the skis, to start the slowing of my rapid orbital speed. To my delight the pointer on my watch showed this procedure to be correct. In fact the stormy time I'd just had of it did not seem to have reversed the needle's progress. In terms of the full circuit, I still had about a tenth of the way to go. By now I believed the reading of the pointer referred to distance, not to difficulty. So, although the journey might be nine-tenths over in distance, there could still be really major troubles ahead. With my supply of gas essentially exhausted, this was a discouraging thought.

Using my magnetic gun I could see another auroral 'ball of wool.' If I hadn't wasted the first discharge of gas, I could simply have switched off the current flow, and then fallen through it. Now I had to navigate through its intricacies—and to do so without error. The mountainous wave structure through which I had to slide and slip was no worse than before, except that on this occasion no mistake at all could be made.

I came through the obstacle with an intense concentration, willing myself to retain control. No longer blinded by any background light, I could use the magnetic gun quite freely. In fact I came through the obstacle without disaster. Yet disaster had been desperately close, for shortly thereafter the magnetic gun refused to function any more.

I ran now into a long wavy structure, fortunately without knots and twists, so that I could ease myself through without real physical difficulty. The mental difficulty was ever present, however, because I now had no means of reassuring myself about the route ahead. I was travelling blind. Not until then did I realise how fully I had come to rely on the few simple gadgets with which I had been equipped. Having recently relied so heavily on the magnetic gun, I felt woefully exposed without it.

The running became smoother. I tried various angles of backward tilt, seeking for the optimum deceleration rate, but to my dismay nothing I did made any difference to the indicator needle. How then was I to know how much to slow down?

My variations did have some effect, however. The more I lay back, the more intense the helically twisted blue-violet flame of the surrounding gas cloud became. This was strange indeed. It was also strange that changing the current flow seemed to make little or no difference. In fact nothing much that I could do made any difference to the pressure on the skis.

The sickening thought that some fault had developed in the current mechanism crossed my mind. Suddenly a light appeared ahead of me, at first a pinpoint like a star. Thinking for a moment that in some way I had managed merely to turn in a huge arc back towards the brilliance I'd managed to avoid only a short time ago, I glanced in desperation at my watch, to find the pointer almost at full circuit.

My fear slowly diminished as I now found the way easy and smooth, totally in contrast to my previous journey. A glowing radiance lay ahead of me, growing quickly from a seeming point to a small disk and then to an appreciable ball.

The ball continued to grow, until it filled the sky, as Jupiter had done. It glowed everywhere, with an inner iridescence. You didn't just see a bright-coloured outer surface. It was as if you could see right inside, except whenever you tried to distinguish anything in detail it immediately disappeared. It was as if an inner something was there, constantly forming, melting away, and then reforming again.

My route now carried me smoothly towards the incandescent area. It was not the same as before, for there was no magnetic 'ball of wool' here. I approached the iridescent region and then was suddenly inside it. The sensation was of being inside a glorious world of light and colour, and with this sensation came the certainty that someone was talking to me. Although I was not conscious of hearing any known words, I knew that I could remove my headpiece. I moved on closer, gliding through the sea of shimmering light. Voices spoke at me now from every side. It wasn't like ordinary speech. It was more like the voices of music. I felt I knew something both beautiful and profound was being said, but that I lacked a knowledge of the language. The sounds became louder as I proceeded.

There were shapes too, showing more clearly the forming and reforming process I'd seen from the outside.

The voices drew me on ever further, and the further I travelled the clearer the shapes became and the more distinctive the sounds. The language seemed not only accessible but immediately within my grasp. Suddenly I knew the language would indeed become clear—but only if I were to proceed beyond the threshold of my own being.

Without hesitation I continued over the threshold into the world of the incandescent ones. In the brief moment before my consciousness dissolved into a vastly greater awareness, I knew that at last I had come home.